"Strasser's writing puts the reader in the midst of the projects and offers totally real characters . . . riveting."
—*VOYA*

"Tight plotting and a crisp style will satisfy readers looking for nonstop action and plenty of urban drama."
—*School Library Journal*

"Hopeful and heartbreaking."
—*Booklist*

IF I GROW UP

TODD STRASSER

SIMON & SCHUSTER BFYR

NEW YORK   LONDON   TORONTO   SYDNEY

To Lia, who helped open my heart,
and Geoff, who helped open my eyes.

SIMON & SCHUSTER BFYR
An imprint of Simon & Schuster Children's Publishing Division
1230 Avenue of the Americas, New York, New York 10020

SIMON & SCHUSTER BFYR is a trademark of Simon & Schuster, Inc.
For information about special discounts for bulk purchases, please contact
Simon & Schuster Special Sales at 1-866-506-1949 or
business@simonandschuster.com.
The Simon & Schuster Speakers Bureau can bring authors to your live event.
For more information or to book an event, contact the Simon & Schuster
Speakers Bureau at 1-866-248-3049 or visit our website
at www.simonspeakers.com.
Also available in a Simon & Schuster Books for Young Readers
hardcover edition.
Book design by Lucy Ruth Cummins
The text of this book was set in Scala.
Manufactured in the United States of America
First Simon & Schuster Books for Young Readers paperback edition February 2010
10 9 8
The Library of Congress has cataloged the hardcover edition as follows:
Strasser, Todd
If I grow up / Todd Strasser.
p. cm.
Summary: Growing up in the inner-city projects, DeShawn is reluctantly forced
into the gang world by circumstances beyond his control.
Includes bibliographical references (p. 221-222)
ISBN 978-1-4169-2523-1 (hc)
1. Gangs—Fiction. 2. Violence—Fiction. 3. Inner Cities—Fiction. 4. Poverty—
Fiction. 5, African Americans—Fiction.] 1. Title.
PZ7.S899 If 2009
[Fic]—dc22
2008000655
ISBN 978-1-4169-9443-5 (pbk)
ISBN 978-1-4391-5663-6 (eBook)

ACKNOWLEDGMENTS

Behind the bling and the glowering crossed-arm poses of rappers are poignant lyrics filled with pain and anguish. Not since the antiwar folk songs of my youth have I heard such intense anger and frustration in music. And no wonder. For a significant number of minorities in this country, life, at best, promises to be little more than decades spent at menial low-paying jobs that ultimately enable others to reap the financial benefits. It's true that there will always be a few exceptions—the entrepreneur, the politician, the actor, music or sports star—but for each one of them there will also be hundreds of thousands of undereducated and disadvantaged souls trapped in an endless cycle of hopelessness and despair. This acknowledgment is for all the rappers and poets who speak out against the way things are, to let them know that people are listening.

PREFACE

In my last book, *Boot Camp*, I wrote about a secret prison system for teenagers in the United States. Teens do not have to be found guilty of a crime to be sent to one of these facilities, also known as boot camps. All they have to be is under the age of eighteen and have parents or guardians who want to send them away.

There is yet another system of detention in our country that holds not thousands, but millions, of innocent people against their wills. Unlike boot camps, which are often located in remote parts of the landscape, these social and economic gulags are hidden in plain sight, often in inner cities, but also anywhere that young people are denied the basic social, economic, and educational opportunities necessary to succeed.

Like many Americans, I believe that the United States provides its citizens with some of the greatest educational, social, and financial opportunities on Earth. But those opportunities are not shared equally. Today significant numbers of American citizens—

mostly minorities, and many living in impoverished inner-city areas—are doomed to fail before they have the chance to embrace the possibilities for a happy and rewarding life that so many of the rest of us enjoy.

For those of us who live in suburbs, small towns, and in the better parts of urban areas, the impoverished inner cities are portrayed by the media as a cauldron of moral decay and crime that now and then produces a talented athlete or music star. We forget that millions of inner-city denizens are just like us—well-meaning human beings who yearn for the simple and basic privileges our country promises: a decent education, a job with a chance for advancement, and a safe place to raise children.

When those privileges are denied, or are unattainable, young men and women seek other avenues to satisfy their needs and fulfill their dreams. This, many believe, accounts for the steady increase in gang membership that has occurred over the past three decades. It is important to note that gang membership knows no ethnic or racial bounds. In addition to Hispanic, African-American, and Asian gangs, it is currently estimated that close to 30 percent of gang membership in smaller cities and rural communities is Caucasian.

Still, the majority of gang members in this country are minority city dwellers. As Malcolm W. Klein states in his book *The American Street Gang: Its Nature, Prevalence, and Control*, "Street gangs are an amalgam of racism, of urban underclass poverty, of minority and

youth culture, of fatalism in the face of rampant depri-
vation, of political insensitivity, *and the gross ignorance
of inner-city . . . America on the part of most of us who do
not have to survive there.*" (My italics.)

Since the dawn of the human race, we have banded
together to improve our chances of survival. It seems
to be basic to our nature. Given this, perhaps we can
understand why, when faced with hopelessness, racism,
and inescapable poverty, young inner-city men are likely
to join gangs.

Perhaps the saddest, most sinister, and devastating
aspect of gangs is that, in the absence of positive influ-
ences, opportunities, and role models, they recruit basi-
cally good, constructive, and naturally well-meaning
young men (and to a lesser degree, young women) and
turn them bad.

This is the story of one of those young men.

TWELVE YEARS OLD

The divisions between black and white, and rich and poor, begin at birth and are reinforced every day of a child's life.

"SOME ASK US WHY WE ACT THE WAY WE ACT WITHOUT LOOKIN' HOW LONG THEY KEPT US BACK."
—FROM "RIGHTSTARTER (MESSAGE TO A BLACK MAN)" BY PUBLIC ENEMY

A SHORTY FALLS

The shouting and screaming outside started at dinner-time. We were sitting on the living room couch, eating macaroni and cheese, and watching *Judge Joe Brown* on the TV. Between the banging of the heat pipes and the noise outside, it was one big racket.

"DeShawn, turn up the sound," Gramma said. I put my tray on the couch and turned up the volume. The TV was old, and no one knew where the clicker was anymore. It was just me and Gramma that night. My big sister, Nia, was out with her boyfriend, LaRue.

Outside the yelling got louder and the police sirens started. Gramma flinched and put down her fork. She shook her gray head wearily, and the skin around her eyes wrinkled. "Noise around here is gonna make me lose my mind."

I glanced toward the thick green curtains that covered the window. Ever since gangbangers cocktailed the apartment down the hall, Gramma had kept the curtains closed all the time.

"Don't go near that window," she warned. "They could start shootin'."

The curtains already had two bullet holes the size of bottle caps. There were bullet holes in the walls, too. Gramma had put a picture over one of them, and another was blocked by our little Christmas tree decorated with tinsel and candy canes. We would have been safer living on a high floor, but the elevators were always broken and it was hard for Gramma to climb the stairs after cleaning houses all day. In the projects, the older you got, the closer to the ground you wanted to live.

The sirens and shouting grew louder. I gave Gramma a pleading look.

"No," she said firmly.

"But the police are here," I argued. "Won't be any more shooting."

"I said no," Gramma repeated, but her words sounded weary and defeated, and I knew I could wear her down.

"Come on, *please?*" I pestered. Outside the sirens had now stopped, but there was still lots of shouting. "Just let me look."

"Oh, okay." Gramma gave in just like I knew she would. "But be quick."

I hurried over and peeked through the curtains. The window was streaked with dirt, and cold winter air seeped in around the edges. Outside a crowd of people had gathered in the dark. All I could see were the tops of heads and shoulders. "Must be something big going on," I said. "Let me go see. *Please?*"

"No! You ain't allowed out after dark."

"I'll stay right by the front, I promise."

"No."

"Nothing bad's gonna happen with all those people out there."

"No!"

"Come on, Gramma, I'll only be a few minutes. I swear."

She let out a disheartened sigh. "You ain't gonna stop botherin' me till I say yes, are you? Come back quick, hear? And don't go nowhere else."

I grabbed my coat, went out into the graffiti-covered hall, down the pee-smelly stairs, across the bare lobby, and through the dented metal doors to the outside. Cold, dark air filled my lungs. The crowd was still growing. Fearful of being trampled, I went behind the mob where it wasn't packed so tightly. There I found Lightbulb, walking in a circle with his eyes squeezed shut and his fingers in his ears. He wore a black wool cap pulled down over his head, and a ratty, old-man-size coat that dragged on the ground.

"S'up Bulb?" I asked.

Lightbulb opened his eyes but shook his head and kept his fingers in his ears. He'd gotten his nickname because of his light skin and the shape of his head. Sometimes he wasn't right in the head, either.

"Come on, don't get all janky on me," I said.

"A shorty fell." Lightbulb winced as if just talking about it caused him pain. "Long way down. He's dead for sure."

By the age of twelve, seeing dead folks was nothing new. The gangbanger who lay glassy-eyed in a pool of blood in the lobby. The lady who was stabbed and crawled down four flights of stairs, leaving a long, brownish red trail before she bled out. The crusty old wino who froze to death on a bench. But I'd never seen a dead kid before.

The crowd was packed tight. No way someone my size could fight through all those legs and hips to see. Besides, the police were lining the area with yellow crime-scene tape. The ambulance men were in there, crouching down. I figured the best place to see would be from the monkey bars in the middle of the yard.

The bars were cold in my bare hands as I climbed. Around me rose the broad, flat buildings of the Frederick Douglass Project. Lights glowed in some windows and red and green Christmas lights were strung across a few balconies, but many more windows were boarded up and dark.

I was watching the police clear a semicircle of space near the side of my building when behind us on Abernathy Avenue, a car door slammed. A black Mercedes with dark windows stood at the curb, shiny chrome rims still spinning like they were going a hundred miles an hour. A man got out and the crowd began to part as he walked toward the building. He was shorter than some, but stocky and powerfully built. There was only one person who commanded that kind of respect: Marcus Elliot, the leader of the Douglass Disciples.

He wore black slacks and a black leather jacket over a white turtleneck sweater, with a big gold chain hanging in front. An earring glimmered. His brown hair was short and neatly trimmed, and he had a square face and small, deep-set eyes that were almost always in a suspicious squint. The crowd quieted and parted, and even the police stepped aside. Marcus stopped and looked over the shoulders of the ambulance men. He stood there for a long time.

The monkey bars rattled as Lightbulb climbed up. His pants were torn at the knees, and the sleeves of his big coat hung down past his hands. Sitting beside me, he started rocking back and forth. Near us, one of the ambulance men came though the crowd with something long and black.

"What's that?" Lightbulb whispered.

"Body bag," I whispered back. "Go find out who fell."

Lightbulb shook his head.

"For a Snickers bar," I said.

"Lemme see."

"It's upstairs. Give it to you tomorrow."

Lightbulb climbed down and disappeared. Meanwhile the ambulance men lifted the body bag onto a stretcher and rolled it through the crowd. The bag was mostly flat, except for a bump in the middle. Marcus walked behind them. His face was hard and flat. Jaws clenched, lips tight. Not a handsome face, but one that said he wasn't afraid of anyone or anything.

Lightbulb climbed back up. "It was Darnell."

Darnell was Marcus's little nephew. I twisted back toward Abernathy Avenue. They'd opened the rear ambulance door to slide in the stretcher. The light from inside reflected on the men's faces. You might have expected that Marcus would be looking down at his nephew. But he wasn't. He was staring back at the project with a look as cold and angry as I'd ever seen.

MARCUS

Darnell's momma was Laqueta, who was Marcus's sister and my best friend Terrell's first cousin. I didn't know who Darnell's father was, only that Laqueta's new boyfriend was Jamar, the Disciples' second in command, and that they lived up on the fifteenth floor. Everyone said Laqueta was the prettiest girl in the projects, with her big round eyes and straight white teeth and constant smile. At least, until the Gentry Gangstas threw Darnell off the roof.

The next morning, Gramma made me put on a heavy coat, gloves, and a hat before I could take my bike outside. Despite the cold, I liked riding around because the ground was hard and you could go almost anywhere in the project. Not like in the spring when the yard was soft and muddy.

Outside, something lay on the ground about thirty feet from the yellow-taped crime-scene spot where Darnell had fallen, far enough away that it might have been missed by the crowd in the dark the night before. It was a window guard, bent in the middle, as if someone had kicked it out of a window frame.

"This where that little boy fell?" a voice behind me asked. I turned. It was a girl with big, pretty eyes, wearing a clean pink jacket with a hood lined with white fur pulled tightly around her face like an Eskimo.

"Over there." I pointed toward the yellow tape.

"It's so sad."

"They say the Gentry Gangstas did it," I said, repeating what I'd heard.

The girl scowled. "Who's that?"

It was hard to believe she didn't know. "The rival gang," I said. "From over in the Gentry Project. I heard Jamar, the baby momma's boyfriend, told the police he saw two men run away wearing green bandanas. That's a Gangsta color."

We were in the shadow of the building where it was cold enough to see our breath come out white. A dozen yards away, in the bright sunlight, was a bench. I walked my bike toward it, and the girl and I told each other our names and ages. Hers was Precious, and like me, she was twelve. The wooden seat on the bench was broken, so I hopped up on the top. Precious stood in front of me with her hands in her pockets. The sun was strong and took some of the icy sting out of the air.

"Where'd you get that nice jacket?" I asked.

"My daddy gave it to me for Christmas." She had a bright smile that reminded me of Laqueta.

"Oh, yeah?" I hardly knew anyone who had a father at home. Much less one who gave gifts. "Only Christmas isn't till next week."

"I got it early 'cause it's cold and I don't have anything else warm."

My best friend, Terrell Blake, came out with his bike. He was wearing baggy pants and an extra-large gray hoodie that hung down to his knees. He rode with one hand, the other jammed down into the hoodie's pocket.

"How come they let you out?" I asked, knowing he was supposed to be inside grieving for Darnell with his family.

"It's too sad and stuffy up there," he said, straddling his bike. "Makes my asthma act up." Terrell was taller than me, with skin a little lighter and a thinner nose. One of his front teeth was chipped from a rock fight we'd had a few months before. Recently he'd started to let his hair grow, and it was almost long enough to braid. He eyed my new friend.

"This is Precious," I said. "She lives in Number Three."

Number Three was the building across the yard from ours. Until that year, my friends and I had stayed close to our own building, warned by our families not to venture too far because we might get caught in the cross fire of gangs shooting. But now we were older and more daring.

We were talking to Precious when Marcus's Mercedes pulled up to the curb on Abernathy Avenue. It was rare to see gangbangers that early in the day. Glancing around warily, the leader of the Disciples started toward us. Marcus's expression was intense and serious all the time. You never saw him joking or clowning. As he got close, I could see the small tattoo of a tear at the corner of his right eye. For people on the outside, the tear was supposed to mean someone close to you had been killed. But in the projects, we knew differently—that tear really meant you had killed someone.

Terrell straightened up. "Uh, hi, Cousin Marcus." His voice quavered.

Marcus barely acknowledged the greeting. "Watch my car," he said. He'd started toward our building when I blocked his path with my bike.

Marcus stopped and scowled at me.

"There's something you should see. Over here," I said, and led Marcus to the window guard. Terrell got on his bike and trailed behind until Marcus swung around. "I tell you to come?" he asked sharply.

Head bowed, Terrell rode back to the bench. In the cold shadow of the building, Marcus picked up the window guard and stared up at the highest floors where Laqueta lived with Jamar and Darnell. Then he looked at me. "DeShawn, right? Raven's son?"

"Yes, sir."

"Anyone else know about this?"

I shook my head. "No, sir."

Marcus slowly squeezed the window guard until it doubled over. The skin of his dark hands tightened and his knuckles bulged. The metal creaked until it formed a *V*, like the *V* in the furrows of skin between his eyes as he fixed them on me. "Know what happens to kids who snitch to the police?"

"Uh-huh."

"I can trust you?"

I nodded. "What about Darnell?"

"I'll take care of that," Marcus said. "Meanwhile this is our secret, understand?"

I understood.

IF I GROW UP

"Who was that?" Precious asked when I returned to the bench where she was talking to Terrell.

Her eyes widened when we told her. "You Disciples?"

"Not yet," Terrell answered.

Even in the sun, the cold gradually seeped through your clothes. Precious shivered and hugged herself. "You want to come to my place and watch TV?"

It was tempting. Neither Terrell nor I had ever been invited into a girl's home before.

"Maybe another time," I said. Terrell scowled at me, and I nodded toward Marcus's car. The corners of my friend's mouth turned down.

Precious's pretty lips pursed. "See you later." She started across the yard toward her building.

Terrell and I rode around the yard, always keeping Marcus's car in sight. I asked him how Laqueta was, and he said she'd cried all night.

"Jamar stay with her?" I asked.

Terrell shook his head. He got off his bike and started sliding around on a frozen puddle, leaving white scratches in the dirty, brownish ice. "If I grow up, I'm gonna have a ride like Marcus's," he said through chattering teeth. He must've been freezing, wearing only that hoodie. "And chains and bling like you wouldn't believe. You know Rance got a solid gold chain that weighs five pounds?"

"How do you know that?" I asked. Rance Jones was the leader of the Gentry Gangstas. I'd never seen him, and I was pretty sure Terrell hadn't either.

"I heard from someone," Terrell said. "And he got a twenty-five-karat diamond pinkie ring. Them Gangstas use kids nine, ten years old."

"Maybe you should join them Gangstas," I joked.

Terrell gave me a sour look. "Marcus is my first cousin. He should let me join the Disciples."

"And get jumped in?" I asked. To prove you'd be loyal to the gang, you had to let yourself be beaten up and burned with cigarettes.

Terrell shrugged. "Everybody else been through it."

On Abernathy Avenue, a police cruiser stopped behind Marcus's car. The window went down, and Officer Patterson wagged a thick, brown finger at us. He was the only person I'd ever heard of who'd grown up in Frederick Douglass and become a cop. I slipped off the bench and went to see what he wanted.

"How you doing, DeShawn?" he asked. He had a round face and a thick, bushy mustache. Growing up, he'd known my mother, and he always said hello when he saw me.

"Okay." I leaned in the open window. The car smelled

like coffee. A shotgun and a computer were mounted next to the driver's seat. Officer Patterson nodded at the Mercedes. "Marcus was that little boy's uncle, right?"

"Yes, sir."

"Give him my condolences, okay?"

"What's that?"

"Tell him I'm sorry about his nephew."

"Yes, sir."

Officer Patterson took a sip of coffee from a paper cup and brushed his mustache with the back of his hand.

"Gonna join the Disciples someday?"

"No, sir. Gonna stay in school and out of trouble."

"Good boy." Officer Patterson reached over and patted me on the shoulder. Then he drove off. I went back to the bench.

"What do you talk to him for?" Terrell asked.

"He knew my momma."

We huddled on the bench, shivering. The three identical buildings in the Frederick Douglass Project loomed up like dirty tombstones. Half the windows were boarded over with wood. The grounds around the buildings were either cracked concrete walks covered with broken glass, or hard-packed, bare, brown dirt with a few trees and some dead brown weeds.

Benches lined the walks, but they were mostly broken. Same with the playground. There were no swings on the swing set, just rusty chains hanging down from the top. The seesaw was gone. What little sand was left in the sandbox was the color of dark smoke. Only the rusty monkey bars remained. As shorties, we used to play on them for hours and then go home with burnt red palms.

We waited until Marcus came back, then, shivering cold, we hurried inside. The lobby was lit by one long, flickering bulb. The mailboxes in the wall had all been busted open by drug fiends looking for welfare checks. The walls were covered with colorful, loopy graffiti and the black slashes of Disciples' tags. Here and there someone had hung a small Christmas wreath or a bunch of holly outside a door.

The elevator was broken as usual, so we carried our bikes up the stairs. Some floors smelled of cooking. Others smelled of weed. On some floors you heard loud TV. On others, rap and hip-hop. And always in the winter, the banging of the heat pipes day and night, like a prison gang eternally busting rocks.

Taped on the wall of each landing was a blue sheet of paper saying that Darnell's funeral would be at one p.m. on Saturday at the First Baptist Church.

Leaving my bike in my apartment, I helped Terrell carry his upstairs. The door to the Blakes' apartment was open, and inside it was hot and crowded with grown-ups. Even though it was the dead of winter, the windows were partway open and women sat fanning themselves. The few men—there were always way fewer men than women—dabbed their foreheads with handkerchiefs.

On a table in the middle of the living room were

plates of food and vases of flowers. It was getting toward the end of the month and, for a lot of people, food was running low. That was especially true around Christmas when there were presents to buy. The sight and smell of those heaping plates made my stomach growl.

Terrell's cousin Laqueta—Darnell's mother—was sitting in the middle of the couch, wearing an old, yellow housedress and clutching a tissue. Her eyes were puffy and red from crying. Terrell's mother, Mrs. Blake, sat on one side of her, and his aunt Rosa sat on the other. Other than Marcus, I'd never heard that Laqueta had any other family.

When Mrs. Blake saw her son, she opened her arms wide. Terrell hesitated and glanced around as if embarrassed to be treated like a little boy. But then he stepped forward and let her hug him. "Terrell," she said in a sad voice. "You're the only good man that's left."

She was looking over Terrell's shoulder at Jamar when she said that. Laqueta's boyfriend sat with his elbows on his knees and his head hanging, a tear tattoo beside each eye. He was tall and rangy, with hair split into cornrows. In his left ear was a big diamond stud, and his hands were covered with gold rings and tattoos. He raised his head and blinked hard, as if trying to squeeze out tears that weren't there. "If only I hadn't left him alone," he said woefully.

People heard him, but no one said anything.

SHOOTING

During the day, the cops and housing police came around, but as soon as it got dark, they were gone. Sometimes gangbangers shot at cops at night or dropped broken TVs on patrol cars or threw bottles out the windows at them. If Gramma had her way, I'd be a house boy—allowed outside only to walk to and from school.

That night Gramma watched *Sanford and Son* and laughed so hard she had to take the tissue out of her sleeve and dab her eyes.

"How can you laugh like that?" I asked. "You've seen this episode a hundred times."

"Something got to make me laugh," Gramma said, still jiggling. "After what happened to that little boy."

Pop! Pop! Pop! Outside they started shooting. It sounded more like cap guns than the big bangs you heard on the TV. Next thing I knew, Gramma was down on the floor next to me and I smelled her perfume. She raised her head alertly. "Where's Nia?" she asked, even though we both knew she was with her boyfriend, LaRue.

Pop! Pop! Crash! More shots, and somewhere nearby a window shattered. *Bang.* A door slammed downstairs, and we heard rapid steps coming up. A key jiggled in the lock and Nia rushed in. My sister was fourteen and had long, straight brown hair and, almost always, a smile. She was breathing hard, and her face was flushed from running. But her eyes gleamed with excitement.

Gramma propped herself up on her elbows. "Get down!" she commanded.

Still gasping for breath, Nia dropped to one knee.

"You're gonna get yourself killed someday," Gramma muttered, even as she relaxed knowing that Nia was safe.

"Those boys shoot all the time," Nia scoffed.

"You forget how your momma died?" Gramma snapped. "How many times I have to tell you not to run when they shoot? You could run right into the cross fire. You hear shootin', you drop to the ground and stay there."

"And get my clothes all dirty?" My sister shook her head.

The shooting stopped. The TV was still on, and Redd Foxx's gravelly voice and the laugh track lured Gramma back to the couch. Nia flopped down and put her arms around Gramma's neck and hugged her.

"DeShawn," my sister said. "Turn the channel to BET."

"Hey!" Gramma started to protest.

"Oh, come on," Nia said with a laugh. "You seen

Sanford and Son so many times, you know it by heart."

I grinned at Gramma. "*Told* you."

"You two are too smart for your own good," she grumbled.

Pop! Pop! Pop! The shooting started again, but now it sounded far away. Gramma stiffened but then looked at Nia and me and relaxed. We were safe. At least for tonight.

WEAPONS

Gramma's apartment had one bedroom with one bed, which she and Nia shared. I slept on the living room couch. On most mornings, Gramma left to clean houses before we woke up. After breakfast Nia and I washed the dishes and put them in the rack to dry. On TV, people had kitchens with dishwashers and bathrooms with showers, but all we had were sinks and a bathtub. Sometimes I'd go into the bathroom and find Gramma on her knees, washing clothes in the tub. There'd once been washing machines in the basement of our building, but they'd been broken so often, the city took them out.

Outside, Terrell and Lightbulb were waiting for me in the yard. In the spot where Darnell fell, someone had stuck a small wooden cross in the dirt, with candles and bunches of flowers around it. The yellow crime-scene tape lay twisted and trampled on the ground. The three of us stared at the cross without speaking. Then Lightbulb said, "You got that Snickers bar?"

I gave it to him, and he tore it open while we walked to school. Terrell turned the bill of his cap to the right and stuck in his gold earring. Ahead of us, Nia and her boyfriend, LaRue, waited on the sidewalk. They were in eighth grade. LaRue was slim with light chocolate skin and almond-shaped eyes, as if he had some Asian blood. His thick black hair was long with lots of loose dreadlocks. The bill of his cap was turned to the right and a black bandanna poked out of his back pocket.

"Terrell," he called. "Com'ere."

My best friend practically bounded over. He didn't have those cool, slow moves yet like the older guys. He and LaRue went behind some parked cars. When they came back, Terrell was arranging the front of his hoodie.

"What'd he give you?" I asked when we started walking again.

Terrell told Lightbulb to get lost. Our friend hunched his shoulders like his feelings were hurt, then went off. Terrell opened the pocket of his hoodie just enough for me to see the gray handle of a box cutter inside.

"Are you whack?" I hissed.

"I'm just gonna take it inside and give it back to him," Terrell said.

"They find it, you'll get expelled," I said. "And what do you think LaRue's gonna do with it in school?"

Terrell shrugged as if he didn't care. "All I know is he said he'd put in a good word for me to Marcus." He took out his asthma inhaler. He seemed to need it whenever he got nervous or excited.

Lightbulb joined us again and we continued to school. Washington Carver was on the border between

Frederick Douglass and the Gentry Street Project. To the school's builders, that must've made sense, because kids from both projects could go to it. But the location also put the school in the middle of the war zone between the Disciples and the Gangstas.

Like a jail, our school had metal bars on all the doors and windows and a tall metal fence that circled the grounds. The sixth graders went in a different entrance than the seventh and eighth graders, whose bags were scanned and bodies were sometimes searched. The sixth graders were rarely searched.

At the sixth-grade entrance stood Ms. Rodriguez, the assistant principal, as ancient as the history in our history books. Her short hair was completely white, and she was all wrinkled skin and gristle. Her job in the morning was to make sure only kids who went to Washington Carver entered, and not any troublemakers from someplace else.

While we waited to go in, Terrell began wheezing again. He took out his inhaler and breathed in deeply. Then it was our turn. At the doorway, Ms. Rodriguez narrowed her eyes at my friend, whose hands were both jammed into the pockets of his hoodie.

"What have you got there, Terrell?" she asked.

CLOWNING

Terrell began trembling, and even though I'd done nothing wrong, I felt nervous and scared too.

My friend sputtered anxiously. "I—"

"Don't give me explanations," Ms. Rodriguez snapped. "Just show me what's in that pocket."

Still trembling, Terrell slowly drew his hand from his pocket.

In it was his inhaler.

Ms. Rodriguez's expression softened. "You okay, honey?"

Terrell nodded and she waved us in.

Inside school my friend grinned devilishly. "Thought I was gonna get busted, right?"

"So did you," I said.

He shook his head. "Nah, I was just foolin' around." He went down the hall toward the cafeteria.

"Where's he going?" Lightbulb asked.

"Nowhere good," I said.

It seemed like everything in Washington Carver was held together with tape. The cracks in the grimy windows, the pages in the tattered old textbooks, the pull-down maps in the front of the room—all held in place with yellowed, peeling tape.

The only things new at school were the teachers. Every year at least half the faces were different. Take Mr. Brand, for example. He had light brown hair, greenish eyes, and copper skin. He spoke proper, not ghetto, and wore button-down shirts, and slacks with cuffs. He was average height but rail thin, because, he said, he ran marathons.

"Settle down, everyone," he said at the beginning of class. "Open your textbooks to page two hundred and eighty-five. Who can tell me why the pyramids were built?"

There were more than forty kids in the class and not enough desks, so some of us had to share. The chubby Douglass kid we called Bublz raised his hand. "Hey, Mr. Brand, is the reason you like ancient history so much because the Egyptians ran marathons like you do?"

"The Greeks ran marathons, not the Egyptians," Mr. Brand replied patiently.

"My book ain't got a page two hundred eighty-five," complained a girl named Ikea.

"Then share with someone else," said Mr. Brand.

"Hey!" said a big, tough Gentry boy named Antwan. "I didn't know them Egyptians were brothers!"

"What'd you think, dummy?" said Bublz. "They come from Africa."

"No, they don't," said Antwan. "They come from Egypt. That's why they're called Egyptians, stupid."

"You're stupid," Bublz shot back. "Where you think Egypt is?"

"In Egypt, retard," said Antwan. "And Africa's in Africa."

Bublz shook his head wearily. "If you were any dumber, they'd have to give you a brain transplant."

Bublz and Antwan were engaged in the daily ritual of clowning. At the beginning of the year, Mr. Brand would tell kids to quiet down, but they would ignore him and continue sassing each other, seeing how far they could push our teacher before he blew. It took a couple of weeks, but Mr. Brand finally exploded, ranting and yelling at the class, which was exactly what they wanted.

After a while, though, Mr. Brand figured out that if he let the class mess around for a time, they might get bored and eventually let him teach. Some days it worked, some days it didn't. A week like this, before a big vacation like Christmas, was usually a lost cause.

In a moment of quiet, Mr. Brand saw a chance to step in. "Who can tell Antwan the difference between Egypt and Africa?"

A couple of hands went up, including mine.

"DeShawn?" Mr. Brand called.

"Africa's a continent," I said. "Egypt's a country in Africa."

"Where in Africa?" asked Mr. Brand.

"Like, North Africa."

"Well, look at the brains on DeShawn," Antwan said snidely.

"That's enough, Antwan," Mr. Brand said.

Antwan ignored him. "Maybe I'll kick your Douglass butt," he threatened.

Instead of answering, I gave him the steely look I imagined Marcus would use. Only I wondered if Marcus's heart ever beat as nervously as mine was.

"What's that?" Antwan taunted. "You tryin' to look tough? You about as tough as my baby sister."

"I said, that's enough," demanded Mr. Brand. But it didn't matter. The class was waiting for my response.

"I'll see you after school," I muttered.

Everyone oohed and aahhed.

Antwan narrowed his eyes and nodded, as if he accepted the challenge. Meanwhile Terrell motioned to me with a fist under his desk. As best friends, we had sworn to watch each other's backs.

When class ended, Mr. Brand asked me to wait until the others left. When they had, he gave me a searching look. "Are you really going to fight him?"

"If I have to." The truth was, most of the talk was just bluster, to be forgotten as soon as the bell rang.

Mr. Brand shook his head as if it made no sense. "Tell me something, DeShawn. Why do they even bother coming to class?"

"Nothing better to do," I said.

"What about you?"

I wasn't sure how to answer. Gramma said I was a good boy, because I did what I was told. But most of the time I only did that because it was easier than not doing it. Even at twelve I had a pretty good notion that school wasn't the way to succeed. We'd all heard stories about the rich and famous rappers and athletes who'd come from the projects. But you never heard of anyone from the projects who got famous for going to school.

Mr. Brand tapped the eraser of a pencil against his desk. "Have you ever heard of Hewlett Academy?"

"No, sir."

"It's a magnet high school over in Beech Hill," he said. "You'll get a better education there."

"Why can't I get it here?" I asked.

Mr. Brand's eyes darted toward the closed door. He lowered his voice. "Just between you and me, DeShawn. This is a dumping ground for teachers who can't get jobs anywhere else. It's hard to get a good education from bad teachers."

"But Beech Hill's far," I said a little nervously.

"You could take a bus." He could probably tell that I wasn't thrilled by the idea. "Don't want to leave your friends, right? Don't want to leave the comfort and familiarity of the hood."

I nodded.

"DeShawn, what do you think's going to happen if you stay here?"

"Go to Munson, I guess." That was the local high school.

"You know that more than half the kids who enter there don't finish?"

"Doesn't mean I won't," I said.

Mr. Brand's shoulders sagged as if pulled down by the weight of something he knew that I didn't. "DeShawn, listen to me. It's one thing to go to school here with all your friends. But it's different when your crew's dropped out and you're the only one left. It's harder when you're still walking to school each day while your peeps drive around in hot whips. You can understand that, right?"

I nodded again. The second bell rang. It was lunchtime and I started inching toward the door.

"Hold on. I'll write you a pass." Mr. Brand pulled a pad out of his desk and started to write. "I want you to think about Hewlett, okay?" he said, tearing a sheet off the pad. "You're still two years away, but you could start to prepare for the entrance exam. There's a special Saturday program I could help you get into."

"I'll think about it." I reached for the pass, but Mr. Brand held it out of range.

"You're pretty good at telling people what they want to hear, aren't you?" He knew he had me. I couldn't go out into the hall without that pass. I looked into his green eyes.

"You wondering why I even bother?" Mr. Brand asked. "Most of these kids don't want my help, DeShawn.

They're perfectly happy to waste their days clowning around without a thought about the future. But maybe you're different. You're one of the few in this class who reads at grade level. Maybe you're the one who'll really do something with his life. But to do that, you'll need a better education than you'll get here. So you'll think about Hewlett, right?"

I nodded. He placed the pass in my hand, and I headed for the door.

DISAPPOINTMENT

Just before the end of school, they announced a delayed dismissal and all sixth graders were sent to the gym. This happened about once a month, usually because there was going to be a gang fight and the school found out and called the police.

"You think that's why LaRue brought that box cutter?" Terrell asked as we walked down the hall to the gym.

"Shhh!" I pressed my finger to my lips. You never knew who might be listening.

In the gym, kids were standing around in groups or sitting in circles on the floor. Lightbulb sat down with a book and a thick pair of old-man eyeglasses with big brown frames.

"Since when do you need glasses?" I asked.

"They make me look smart," he said.

"You look dumber than Urkel in those things," Terrell said. "Ain't nothing gonna make you look smart."

"Says you," said Lightbulb. Some of the teachers said Lightbulb was a genius.

"What's 145 times 216?" I asked.

Lightbulb closed his eyes and moved his lips. "31,320."

"That right?" Terrell looked at me.

"How would I know?" I said.

Lightbulb read for a while, then took off the glasses and pressed his fingers into the corners of his eyes. "It's hard to see through these things. My head hurts."

"Where'd you get those glasses?" I asked.

"Found 'em."

"You can't just wear any old glasses," I said. "You have to go to a doctor and get them made special."

"For real?" Lightbulb said. He may have been a genius in school, but in some ways he really was the dumbest kid we knew.

"Hey, DeShawn." Terrell nudged me with his elbow. "Someone's checking you out."

A group of giggling girls sat in a circle across the way. One was taller than the others, with long brown hair and sparkling eyes. We'd been exchanging looks for a few weeks.

"She's pretty," said Lightbulb.

Terrell nudged me again. "Go talk to her."

"Back off."

"You scared?"

The truth was, I did want to go. I felt drawn to that tall pretty girl the way Lightbulb was drawn to candy.

"He's going," Lightbulb cheered when I started across the gym.

"Go, DeShawn. Go!" Terrell chanted.

The girls around the tall one grew jumpy with

excitement and began whispering in her ear. Her eyes widened, and then a faint scowl appeared on her face and she turned and shook her head sharply. Suddenly it seemed as if she was annoyed with their chatter, because she got up and came toward me. We met in the middle of the crowded gym.

"Go on, get closer," one of her friends called, and the others cackled.

The tall girl turned to them. "Shush! Shut your mouths." She spoke with authority, and the other girls got quiet. I liked that.

"I'm DeShawn," I said.

"I know," she said, tilting her head toward the other girls. "They told me. I'm Tanisha."

"New here?"

She nodded. Her eyes were glowing.

"Where're you from?" I asked. My heart was fluttering in my chest, but I knew I had to play it cool.

"Over on the east side of town. We moved over the summer."

"How come?" I asked.

She lowered her head and stared at the floor. The reasons for moving to the projects were never good.

"Sorry," I said. "It's none of my business."

She raised her head. "How long've you been around here?"

"All my life. My gramma moved here about thirty years ago."

"Your momma go to this school?"

"Yeah."

"Bet she had Ms. Rodriguez," Tanisha said. "She's so old, *everybody* must've had her."

I laughed. Ms. Rodriguez had been a teacher before she became assistant principal. Tanisha was funny. I liked that, too. "Where do you live now?"

"Gentry," she said.

And just like that we went from hot to cold. From hope to no hope. It didn't matter that I wasn't a Disciple. I was from Frederick Douglass, and if I was seen by Gentry Gangstas on their turf, they would automatically consider me a spy and up to no good. They might not kill me for that, but I was sure to catch a beating.

Sensing that something was wrong, Tanisha frowned.

"Well, nice to meet you," I said, and turned away.

BULLETS

On Christmas morning, Gramma gave me a tight-fitting, fuzzy blue sweater I knew I'd never wear. I gave her and Nia little bottles of perfume that a man on the street had sold me. Nia gave me a DVD of the *Transformers* movie. We ate a Christmas lunch. In the afternoon, I went out and found Lightbulb.

"Where're we going?" he asked as we climbed the piss-smelly stairwell.

"Upstairs," I said.

He stopped. "You crazy? No one but Disciples are allowed up there."

"Shh. . . . Quiet. I need a lookout."

"Who's gonna look out for me?" Lightbulb asked.

"I got a Snickers bar."

The top two floors were Disciples territory. Not that they paid rent. They'd broken through the doors and put on their own locks. They used the apartments as places to live and safe houses for anyone who needed to hide. On the fifteenth floor the stairwell and hallway were covered with loopy tags—TAP and Casper and Baby—and also, everywhere, like religious symbols to ward off evil spirits, was the six-pointed-star symbol of the Disciples.

Pressed against a wall was an old chest of drawers. It didn't make sense for it to be there, and I pushed it aside.

"What're you doing?" Lightbulb asked in a quavering voice.

"Shh . . . " Behind the chest was a hole through the cinder-block wall big enough for someone to crawl through. I bent down and peeked into an empty room with a bare mattress lying on the floor. Giving the Snickers bar to Lightbulb, I said, "You hear anyone come up the stairs, you holler into this hole, then go down the other stairs as fast as you can."

Lightbulb was already tearing open the wrapper. He took a bite and nodded. I crawled through the hole. In the room on the other side, the floor was covered with empty bottles, cigarette butts, magazines, and food wrappers. The bare mattress was stained a dozen different shades of yellow and brown. I crossed the room and stopped at the door to listen. It sounded quiet on the other side, and I slowly opened the door and went down the hall.

About a million cockroaches scattered when I entered the kitchen. It smelled like garbage, and the sink and counters were covered with dirty dishes, empty take-out containers, fried-chicken buckets, and pizza boxes. I opened the cabinet under the sink, and about a million more cockroaches fled. At the back of the cabinet was another hole leading to the next apartment. I'd heard that the holes were so gangbangers could escape if the police raided. In some rooms there were even holes in the floors so they could drop down to another floor and escape that way.

I crawled into the next apartment. This one had a strong chemical smell. In the middle of the living room was a Ping-Pong table with cutting boards, white breathing masks, a couple of small postal scales, and razor blades smudged with yellowish white powder. Hundreds of small Ziploc bags and plastic vials were scattered about.

Piled on the kitchen counter were dozens of empty baking-soda boxes, as well as half a dozen old cooking pots caked with soot—the tools for making crack.

Two apartments later I got to the one where Jamar and Laqueta lived. Terrell said that ever since Darnell died, Laqueta was staying with them on the sixth floor so I knew it would be empty. Unlike the other apartments, this one was clean and had curtains on the windows, nice furniture, and a big TV in the living room. An unfamiliar smell hung in the air, and it took a moment for me to realize it was the pine scent of the Christmas tree in the corner.

I went down the hall to a bedroom with a small bed with brown and green Simba sheets and pillows. Some stuffed animals and toy trucks were on the floor. The window was open, and the blue curtain was half in and half out, so I knew there was no window guard.

Carefully pulling the curtain back, I stuck my head outside.

Down in the yard, people were the size of Tic Tacs, and on the street, cars looked like Matchbox toys. Behind Frederick Douglass was a big rail yard with dozens of tracks and all kinds of trains, and I heard the sharp squeak of metal wheels on rails. Between Frederick Douglass and the yard was a double row of tall chain-link fence with coils of razor wire on top.

I looked at the window frame. In the holes that would have held the window guard were broken, rusty brown screws with shiny silver insides, as if they had just recently snapped. To my mind, it would have taken a hard kick to break those screws.

A lock clacked somewhere in the apartment, and I quickly spun around and ducked down behind a chest of drawers. Through the open doorway, I heard footsteps and the rustle of clothes. My heart started beating hard and my breaths became short and shallow. I knew if I got caught, I might be the next kid to fall fifteen floors.

"You got hollow tips?" a voice asked.

"Dollar each," answered a voice that sounded like Jamar's.

"A dollar each? That's robbery!"

"Take it or leave it," said Jamar.

"Ain't no other place else to get 'em," the other voice said angrily. "You got me right where you want me, don't you? Risking my life to come over here, and you darn well know I can't go back empty-handed."

If Jamar answered, I couldn't hear him. Then the other man said, "I'll take a hundred. And I won't be sorry if one of 'em winds up in the back of your skull."

"Merry Christmas," said Jamar.

A door slammed, but I heard footsteps in the apartment and knew Jamar was still there. I stayed behind the dresser, my heart racing and body tensed. Darn Lightbulb. He was supposed to warn me. Now I was trapped.

Jamar moved around in the other room, whistling and humming to himself. Then the door creaked and closed. I heard the lock click. It sounded like he'd left.

I took a deep breath and felt light-headed with relief. Still I waited a few more minutes before quietly leaving the bedroom and going out into the apartment. On the living room table was an open black and gold box about the size of a small loaf of bread. Inside were bronze and gray bullets.

I crawled through the holes in the apartment walls and back out into the hall. Lightbulb was gone. He probably heard Jamar and the other guy coming up the stairs, got scared, and ran. If any other kid had done that, I would have been mad. But it was hard to be mad at Lightbulb.

DRIVE BY

The First Baptist Church was in a storefront on Belmar Street, at the edge of the area called the Flats. It had once been a pet store, but there'd been a fire and now it was a church with rows of pews and an altar. On damp days the rancid smell of old smoke still hung in the corners.

On the day of Darnell's funeral, the Disciples stood on the sidewalk outside the church, wearing sharp, neatly buttoned gray suits with black shirts and ties. Instead of baseball caps, they wore gray fedoras. Their suits looked new and expensive, and I felt ashamed of the ill-fitting secondhand jacket and slacks Gramma had bought for me at Goodwill. Nia, wearing her frilly, pink Sunday dress, hat, and white gloves, went to LaRue and gave him a kiss, but as I passed the Disciples, I kept my eyes down. The sleeves of my jacket barely reached my wrists, and the bottoms of my gray pants flapped above my ankles. Not knowing how to tie a tie, I'd made up a knot.

At the entrance to the church, a hand came out to stop me. I looked up into the small, hard eyes of Marcus. "Turn around," he ordered.

I did as I was told and felt him press behind me as

he reached over, untied, and retied my tie. The corner of something hard jutted into my back, and I knew at once why all the Disciples had kept their jackets buttoned.

Marcus's hands were quick and sure as he tightened the tie around my neck until I thought I'd choke. Then he placed his strong hands on my shoulders and pointed me inside.

They'd put Darnell in a small, light blue coffin surrounded by bunches of red and yellow flowers. The coffin was open, and people were going up to look. In the front row Laqueta sat with Mrs. Blake and Terrell, dabbing her eyes with a handkerchief. She turned her head and looked to the back of the church, and I realized she was looking at Jamar. Maybe she wanted him to sit with her. But Jamar stood with the other Disciples and didn't move.

Terrell's mom whispered into his ear, and he scanned the crowd until his eyes caught mine. He jerked his head, and I knew he wanted me to go with him to look in the coffin. Like I said before, I'd seen dead people, but never a shorty and when Terrell and I went up to the front I didn't want to look at first. But they'd dressed Darnell in a light blue suit with a white shirt and silver tie and his eyes were closed, so he looked like he was asleep.

"My little cousin," Terrell whispered with watery eyes. I put my hand on his shoulder, and after a moment we went back to our seats.

Pop!

Minister Franklin had barely begun his sermon when the first shot was fired. Hardly anyone looked up. Maybe we were all so used to hearing gunfire that at first it didn't mean anything. But louder shots quickly followed. *Pop! Pop! Pop!* Glass began to shatter and some plaster in the wall exploded. Women started screaming. Minister Franklin ducked down behind the pulpit, and Gramma pushed Nia and me down to the floor between the pews.

The tiles felt cold and gritty. All around us people were on the floor, their eyes squeezed shut and their good clothes getting dirty. *Pop! Pop! Pop!* We could hear the sharp zings and cracks as bullets whizzed overhead, hitting walls and pews. Cold air started floating in through the broken windows.

Then car tires screeched. Footsteps slapped as some of the men ran outside. I slithered along the floor and stuck my head out into the aisle. All that remained of the windows at the front of the church were jagged shards. Outside on the sidewalk, framed by the doorway, Marcus stood tall, his arm straight out, firing a big black gun with slow deliberateness. *Pop! Pop! Pop!*

Then his arm went down to his side, and faint wisps of smoke drifted from the gun's barrel. He looked so powerful in his dark suit. Like some TV hero who wasn't afraid of anyone or anything. A few other

Disciples who'd crouched behind cars and lampposts joined him.

Inside the church people began getting up. Minister Franklin poked his head out from behind the pulpit.

"Damn Gangstas," Nia grumbled angrily as she smoothed out her pink dress and brushed the dirt off.

"How do you know?" I asked.

My sister looked at me like I was stupid. "It's Marcus's nephew in that casket. Besides, who else would shoot up a funeral?"

Marcus came down the aisle, his face squeezed tight with anger. He said something to Minister Franklin and then went outside again.

The minister continued the service. Only now Marcus and the Disciples stood on the sidewalk in case the Gentry Gangstas came back. Cold air filled the church. We pulled our coats on and shivered while Minister Franklin told us how Darnell was with the angels.

THIRTEEN YEARS OLD

Public schools in the United States are becoming more racially segregated, and the trend is likely to accelerate because of a recent Supreme Court decision forbidding most voluntary local efforts to integrate educational institutions.

"CUZ SEE THE SCHOOLS AIN'T TEACHIN' US NOTHIN'
THEY AIN'T TEACHIN' US NOTHIN'
BUT HOW TO BE SLAVES AND HARD WORKERS
FOR WHITE PEOPLE TO BUILD UP THEY [STUFF*]."
—FROM "THEY SCHOOLS"
BY DEAD PREZ
*LYRICS EDITED FOR LANGUAGE

OUT OF THE HOOD

The projects stayed the same, but I changed. I wouldn't be caught dead in the pants and shirts Gramma got from the Goodwill store. Now I wore baggy jeans, big hoodies, and chains like the other guys.

I woke early and quietly dressed. It wasn't even eight o'clock and already the apartment felt hot. In the kitchen the cockroaches scattered from the counters when I turned on the light. After wiping a bowl clean in case roaches had crawled on it during the night, I filled it with Corn Flakes and looked in the refrigerator for milk, but there was none. It was the end of the month. We were out of bread, and there weren't enough powdered eggs left in the box for a meal. This wouldn't be the first time I'd eat Corn Flakes with water.

I was heading for the front door when Gramma shuffled out of the bedroom.

"Where you goin'?" she said.

"Out."

"No, you ain't. Been too much shootin' around here

lately. Now get away from that door." She crossed her arms and waited. But why did I have to listen to her? Who was she anyway? Just some gray-haired woman in a ratty old nightie.

I put my hand on the doorknob.

"You'll be sorry," Gramma warned.

I started to turn the knob, but something was holding me back—all those years of being a good boy, always doing what I was told. "I won't go far. I'll be okay, Gramma, really."

"You don't know what you'll be, child," Gramma said, the veneer of sternness giving way unexpectedly to something sad and defeated. "But I do."

"Just because I'm going out doesn't mean I'll join the Disciples," I said, pulling the door open.

"Just because you're goin' out don't guarantee you'll come back," Gramma muttered.

I hung my head, unable to look her in the eye, but felt a call from outside that I couldn't resist.

The sun was bright and a few people were going to church. The men were in shirtsleeves, and some of the women carried umbrellas to shade themselves. Lightbulb was sitting on the back of the bench nearest our building, writing in a book. A little nappy-haired girl of about eight was playing with a doll in front of the bench. She was wearing a stained, green jumper and had a lollipop in her mouth.

"Hi, Lollipop," I said.

Lightbulb's sister looked up at me and grinned,

some gaps where her baby teeth had fallen out. The lollipop bulged in her cheek.

"You watching her?" I asked Lightbulb.

He nodded. "Till my momma gets back from the store."

I looked over his shoulder. "What's that?"

"Sudokus." He tore a page from the book and gave it to me. The page said EASY, but it wasn't. I worked at it for a while, then got bored and quit. Meanwhile Lightbulb worked on a puzzle in the SUPER HARD part of the book. In no time he'd finished it and turned to the puzzle on the next page. Someone who didn't know him might have thought he was faking, but he wasn't.

The sun rose higher and the day grew hotter. Women came out with babies in strollers and sat in whatever shade they could find. Some older guys squatted near a wall, playing hip-hop on a boom box while they smoked and shot dice. Lightbulb's mom returned and took Lollipop.

Terrell came out wearing a sleeveless white T-shirt, his pants so low it was hard to understand why they didn't slide down to his ankles. He slid his earring into his ear and turned the bill of his cap to the right.

"S'up?" he asked.

"Just chilling."

"Cooking's more like it," Lightbulb said. By now he'd finished all the SUPER HARD puzzles and was wearing the book, opened in the middle, on his head to keep the sun off.

A car horn honked. A police cruiser had stopped at the curb, and inside, Officer Patterson wagged his finger at me. But I didn't move.

"Ain't gonna talk to your friend?" Terrell asked.

Those days were over. Officer Patterson and I exchanged a long look, then he drove back into traffic.

Terrell bounced from foot to foot, jittery like a dope fiend who can't find a fix. Only Terrell was no addict. "I got to get out of here," he said. "Sometimes I just can't take this place one more minute. Look at it. Everything's broken and dead. It's like the last place on Earth."

I knew what he meant. Except for the weeds, the ground was bare and dusty. Broken glass glittered in the sun, and here and there lay a discarded Pampers. Just a few years ago we'd happily run around and played our games here. It never occurred to us that there was anything wrong. But now it was like we'd grown a new set of eyes.

"Want to take a walk?" I asked.

Terrell shook his head. "Too hot. Wish there was some place air-conditioned to go."

"The bus," Lightbulb said.

Terrell grinned. Neither he nor I would have thought of that. "Let's bounce."

"Where?" Lightbulb asked nervously.

"Don't matter," Terrell said. "We'll stay on till it comes back."

We'd spent enough time sitting on the bench

watching traffic to know that sooner or later the buses always came back.

"I better not," Lightbulb said.

"You a momma's boy?" Terrell taunted him.

"No!" Lightbulb insisted.

"Prove it."

Lightbulb looked at me. "You gonna do it, DeShawn?"

I nodded, not letting on that I was probably as nervous as he was. We waited at the bus stop where Gramma stood in the morning when she went to clean houses. When the bus came, Terrell led us through the middle doors, where people usually got off. The three of us squeezed into a seat, and the air-conditioning poured over us like a cool, welcoming breeze.

"Uh-oh." Lightbulb gulped. The driver was frowning in the rearview mirror.

"He won't do nothing," said Terrell. He was right. The bus pulled into traffic, and before long we were in a different world, where the buildings were twice as high as at Douglass and the sidewalks were filled with people jammed so close that it looked like they were brushing shoulders.

Everything looked shiny and new. The stores had sparkling windows without bars, and doors you could simply walk through without being buzzed in. It seemed impossible that all this existed just a dozen blocks from where we lived.

"Man, that's a lot of white people!" Lightbulb blurted.

A fat man in a seat near us chuckled, and Lightbulb

lowered his voice to a whisper. "I never knew there was so many."

"There's way more white people than black," Terrell whispered back. "Look at TV."

"There's plenty of blacks on TV," Lightbulb said.

"Where?" Terrell said. "On BET? Comedy shows? Rap videos? You ever seen *a crowd* on TV? Like at a baseball game? The Olympics or something? It's all white. The only time you see a crowd of blacks, it's got to be a riot."

Terrell had a point, but I understood what Lightbulb meant too. Except for TV and the movies, I'd never seen so many white people. And not a single empty store or vacant lot or boarded-up window was in sight.

People got on and off the bus. Some noticed the three black kids squeezed into one seat, but most didn't. The three of us kept staring out with round, wide eyes. All those tall, clean buildings. All those people hurrying like they had important places to go. It wasn't that I wanted to be part of that world; it seemed strange and foreign. I felt as if they'd spot me right away as someone who didn't belong, who didn't know the right way to act or what to say. They'd shoo me away or maybe even call the police.

But how could that world exist so close to ours?

SOON TO SHOOT

"Where's that toast and olives, DeShawn?" Nia called from the living room.

"Coming up," I called back from the kitchen as I toasted bread in a skillet on the stove.

Tanisha smiled at me and her eyes twinkled. The kitchen was the only place in the apartment where we could get a little privacy. I opened the refrigerator and pulled out the butter, jelly, and olives. It was just past the first of the month, and Gramma's check and food stamps had arrived, so there was plenty of food.

"She eats all day," Tanisha whispered.

"You would too," I whispered back, then headed to the living room where my sister was propped against some pillows on the couch with her hair tied into a dozen little pigtails and her face glistening with a sheen of perspiration. The TV was on loud so she could hear it over the whir of the window fan. Under a big white T-shirt her stomach was swollen to the size of a basketball.

"You're a good brother," she said, shifting uncomfortably and taking the plate from me. She lifted a piece of toast to her lips, then winced.

"What is it?" I asked.

"Nothing. One of 'em just kicked."

"Can I feel?"

My sister gave an irritated groan and nodded. She was getting tired of me asking to feel her stomach, but I was fascinated by how tight and firm the skin of her belly had become as it stretched to encase the new lives growing inside her.

"Okay, that's enough," Nia said when my hand had overstayed its welcome.

"But they didn't kick yet."

"I said, *enough*."

I went back to the kitchen. Tanisha had pulled her hair into a ponytail and lifted it to cool the back of her neck. She wore long, glittering earrings, a white T-shirt, and shorts that showed off her long legs. She gently dabbed her forehead with a folded paper towel, trying not to smudge her makeup.

"I better go," she said.

"Just a little longer." I took her in my arms we kissed. Over the past year, my worries about her being from Gentry had been outweighed by the attraction I felt toward her. Other girls wore sexier clothes and more makeup. They brushed against me in the school halls and gave me inviting looks. But there was something proud and dignified about Tanisha that they didn't have.

She started to wiggle out of my arms. "Lemme go, DeShawn," she breathed hotly in my ear. "If I don't get home soon, my momma's gonna start asking questions." While my family knew about Tanisha, she had not told her family about me. If it weren't for those stupid gangs, there wouldn't have been a problem.

As we left the building, Tanisha slid her hand into mine. I didn't like holding hands in public, but I didn't want to hurt her feelings, either. The afternoon sun had dipped behind Number Three, casting a long shadow across the yard, which was crowded with people escaping from hot, cramped apartments.

"Hey, lover boy!" Terrell and his new crew were hanging around the bench. I pulled my hand from Tanisha's, but it was too late. The guys were grinning. There was the fat kid named Bublz and a kid a year younger than us named Darius, who was small, but wiry and stronger than he looked. They wore their hats backward and three small fake diamonds in the shape of a triangle in their right earlobes. Since Marcus wouldn't let his cousin become a Disciple, Terrell decided to start a junior gang of his own. They sold bootleg CDs and DVDs. As long as they didn't sell drugs or interfere with other Disciple business, Marcus didn't seem to care.

"Going out back?" Terrell yelled with a grin. "Out back" wasn't any place in particular. It was what the older guys said when they were taking a girl somewhere private. Terrell had only said it to impress the other guys, but he shouldn't have been using me to impress them. And he knew it.

He slid off the bench and came toward Tanisha and

me with a swagger in his step. Jerking his head to the side like some kind of hard hitta, he said, "Let's talk." The tough pose annoyed me, but since he was my friend, I gave Tanisha a look that said to wait. Terrell and I walked out of earshot and stopped beside the spot near our building where eight months before, Darnell had fallen to his death. All that was left of the shrine was a piece of wood from the cross and the stub of a red candle.

Terrell pulled a toothpick out of his pocket and slid it between his lips, like Mr. Tough Street Thug. "What're you doing with that Gentry girl?"

I'd had enough of his act. "You know her name. Don't pull this crap with me."

Terrell shook his head. "This ain't no crap. Gentry's the enemy."

"Maybe the Disciples's enemy, but not ours. Besides, she's no Gangsta and I'm no Disciple."

Terrell shifted the toothpick from one side of his mouth to the other and narrowed his eyes at me. The pose was starting to get on my nerves.

"How come you won't get with Soon To Shoot?" he asked.

I glanced at his "crew" around the bench, crossing their arms and lowering their gazes, practicing defiant, menacing looks. "You sure you don't want to call yourselves Soon To Shave?"

Terrell's lower lip jutted out angrily. "The only reason you ain't with us is because of *her*."

"The only reason I ain't with you is because I don't *want* to be with you."

"House boy," Terrell taunted. It was about as bad an insult as you could fling. Already frustrated by not getting to be alone with Tanisha, I felt my fists clench.

Terrell lifted his fists. "Okay, come on, let's see what you got." But as he spoke, his eyes darted back at his crew, and I knew it was just more show. I dropped my fists and started back toward Tanisha. Terrell followed.

"You're messing everything up for me," he said in a hushed voice he didn't want the others to hear. "If you got with us, Marcus might think serious about bringing us into the Disciples."

"How about you get with me and think serious about coming back to Washington Carver?" I asked. School was set to begin in a few days, and Terrell had said he wasn't going back.

Terrell jerked his head at Tanisha, who was talking on her cell phone, her face bright and animated. "Only reason *you* go is 'cause of her."

I spun around and aimed a finger at his face. "For the last time, you leave her out of this. You get with the gangbangers, and all *you're* gonna do is wind up in jail."

"Marcus and Jamar ain't in jail," Terrell said. "They're wearing fresh clothes and driving hot rides. They got more bank and bling than you'll ever get from going to school. All they teach in school is how to work for the white man."

"Stop talking trash." I turned and headed again toward Tanisha.

"Am I?" Terrell asked, following me. "Look at what they teach us. The history of white people. Books by white people. Stay in school and all you'll ever be is a pawn for white people."

"Not me," I said.

Oh, yeah?" Terrell said. "Then what else you gonna be?"

I didn't answer. The truth was, I didn't know.

"Come on, DeShawn," Terrell said behind me. "You know you gotta get with us sooner or later. Around here there ain't nothing else you can do."

SARDINES AND A LOAF

It turned even hotter the next day. Terrell and I were up in his apartment playing Thrill Kill on his Xbox with the window fan blowing on us like a gale. The anger we'd felt the day before had passed, but I wasn't sure our friendship was the same as it had been. Inside we were still a couple of kids playing games, but outside he was an aspiring gangbanger and I wasn't. We were both careful not to mention Tanisha. Terrell paused the game and went over to his desk and took a handful of peanuts in the shell out of a plastic bag.

"Have some," he offered.

"Where'd you get 'em?" I cracked open a shell.

"Cousins in Georgia. They got their own farm."

"Ever been there?"

Terrell shook his head. "What do I want to go to some farm for?"

From outside, above the whir of the fan, came yelling and laughter. I went to the window. Someone had opened a fire hydrant on Abernathy, and bare-chested boys, and girls in T-shirts, were playing in the spray.

"Want to get wet?" I asked.

"And play with shorties?" Terrell asked derisively, his hands working the controller feverishly, his forehead glistening with sweat.

"Who cares?" I said. "Long as we cool off."

Terrell didn't answer. He was busy mowing down bad guys. "I'm gonna get that new PlayStation soon as it comes out."

"Oh, yeah? What bank are you gonna rob?" I asked.

Terrell glanced at the closed door to his room, then pulled a thick wad of bills out of his pocket and fanned them. Mostly fives and tens, and more money than I'd ever seen in one place.

"Where'd you get that?" I whispered.

"Smash 'n' grabs," he answered.

I gave him an uncertain look. Smashing car windows at red lights and grabbing chains off drivers' necks, or pocketbooks from seats, was a serious hustle. But it was hard to imagine how else he could have come up with that much gwap.

There was a knock on the door, and Terrell quickly slid the money back into his pocket. "Who's there?"

The door opened and Laqueta looked in. Her skin was all ashy, her hair nappy, and she was wearing a long, yellow T-shirt with stains on the front. It was hard to believe that she'd once been the prettiest girl in the projects. But that was before Darnell fell.

"Go get me a bottle of Cisco," she said.

"Get lost," Terrell shot back, hunched over his game controller.

"Get me that bottle, or I'll tell your momma how much money you got," Laqueta threatened.

Terrell grit his teeth. Women were not allowed to boss gangbangers—even pretend gangbangers—around.

"Come on," I said. "I want to get out of here anyway."

Passing the stairwell on the fourth floor, we came across a bent old man gripping a walker with bony hands. His hair was white, his yellow eyes were bloodshot, and his skin hung from his face like baggy clothes.

"I need some food." When he spoke, you saw more pink gum than teeth. Tied to the front of the walker was a basket with a few wrinkled dollar bills and some change inside.

"Give me the money," Terrell said. "I'll get you something."

"Not you. Him." The old man pointed a shaky finger at me. "You Shanice's grandson, right? They say you a good boy. I ain't eat in two days. Get me some sardines and a loaf."

"Okay." I reached into the basket and took the money. "What apartment you in?"

"Don't matter," he said. "I'll wait for you here."

"You can't stand here and wait," I said. "Tell me what apartment you're in, and I'll bring it to you."

The old man turned to Terrell. "Go away."

Terrell gave him a contemptuous look, then headed

down the stairwell to the next floor. With his shaky, wrinkled hand, the old man grabbed my shirtsleeve and tugged me close so he could whisper into my ear. His breath smelled god-awful. "Four-G. But don't go tellin' that other boy. He'll break in, steal everything I have."

It was hard to imagine the old man had anything worth stealing, but I agreed just the same.

The closest food store was Wally's. The front was boarded up and covered with colorful graffiti and tags. You wouldn't have thought it was even a place of business unless you knew it was there. Inside, the light was dim and a ceiling fan whirred. The sweet scent of ripe fruit hung in the air. Wally was a big, fat walrus of a man who sat all day by the cash register. People said he kept a sawed-off shotgun under the counter.

"Don't be coming in here to steal," he warned when we entered. He had a green dish towel draped around his fat neck, and his shirt was dark with sweat stains.

"You got sardines and a loaf?" I asked.

"Sardines over there." Wally pointed a fat finger. "Bread over here. Be quick."

We'd hardly taken a step when Wally held out his hand at Terrell. "You buyin' something?"

My friend shook his head.

"Then wait outside," Wally said.

Terrell gave Wally his best narrow-eyed, menacing, hard-hitta look, then left. I got the food and joined him out under the glaring yellow sun. Terrell muttered,

"I'm gonna come back with my boys and bust that place up."

"Why?" I asked.

"You see how he dissed me? Like I was gonna rob the place."

"He treated you like a gangbanger," I said. "I thought that's what you wanted."

We walked a block to the liquor store. The door was always locked. Terrell pushed the buzzer, and we looked up at the security camera so the owner could see our faces. The door buzzed open. Inside was a narrow aisle with walls of thick, scuffed Plexiglas rising to the ceiling. Everything—the cash registers, counters, and shelves of bottles—was behind the Plexiglas.

"What do you boys want?" A woman with red lips and a big head of dyed, reddish orange hair asked through some holes in the thick plastic.

"My cousin Laqueta wants some Cisco," Terrell said.

Recognition softened the woman's expression. "The momma of that little boy who went off the roof last Christmas?"

Terrell nodded and slid some money through a slot. The woman opened a small door in the Plexiglas and pushed through a dark red bottle with a strawberry-colored label.

"Police ask where you got this bottle, what you gonna say?"

"Someone gave it to me," Terrell answered.

"Who?" the woman asked.

"I dunno, some old man," Terrell answered.

The woman made a face. "Now, why would some old man do that?"

"My momma gave it to us," I volunteered. "To bring to his momma."

The woman nodded. "That's right. That's what you say."

Back at Douglass, Terrell took the wine to Laqueta, and I took the food to the old man in 4-G. He asked me if I wanted to come in, but I said no. I knew he was lonely. With the elevator broken, he probably hadn't been downstairs in days or maybe even weeks. I felt bad for him.

When I got to my apartment, LaRue was sitting in the living room with Nia. He was wearing Disciples black.

"Let's bounce," he said.

"Where?" I glanced at Nia, who returned a tight, concerned look.

"Upstairs," LaRue said.

BAIL MONEY

On the fifteenth floor, LaRue stopped outside a door across the hall from the apartments I'd snuck into the previous winter. I could hear a TV inside. LaRue knocked three times, then paused and knocked twice.

Locks clinked, and Marcus opened the door. His broad, flat forehead glistened with sweat, and his T-shirt had dark, wet spots. A white towel hung over his shoulders. Behind him were weights and a bench, and the room was pungent with the scent of sweat. The leader of the Disciples gestured for me to come in and told LaRue he could go. Then he bolted the door shut. I'd lost my nervousness while climbing the stairs, but now it came back. My heart was beating rapidly and my breaths came short and fast. What did Marcus want with me?

"Thirsty?" he asked.

I wasn't, but I was afraid to offend him, so I nodded.

"Check the fridge." He pointed toward the kitchen. "And get me a beer."

The kitchen was clean and neat, the counter lined

with bottles of vitamins and nutrition powders. The refrigerator was filled with malt liquor, wine, six-packs of soda, and energy drinks. I got a beer for Marcus and a Coke for myself. Back in the living room, Marcus was doing curls with the biggest dumbbell I'd ever seen. The skin around his eyes creased, and his jaw clenched. The veins in his forehead and right arm swelled as he lifted the weight over and over, the biceps bulging and relaxing again and again until he let the dumbbell fall to the floor with a thud.

He sat there breathing hard for a few moments, opening and closing the hand that had just held the weight, as if trying to get the blood to flow again. Then he cracked the beer, took a gulp, and nodded at the weight. "Give it a try."

I grabbed the handle with both hands where he had used one, and managed to lift it an inch off the ground before it pulled me back down. I tried again, pulling with all my might, my arms and body trembling under the strain, and got the dumbbell up to my knees.

"Okay," Marcus said.

Thump! The dumbbell hit the floor harder than I'd wanted, and I felt embarrassed. I sat down, clutching the cold soda in my hands, my trembling arms so drained I wasn't sure I could even pop the top off the can.

"When's those babies due?" Marcus asked.

"Two months, I think."

"Nia gonna go live with LaRue, or he gonna move in with you?"

The question caught me off guard. I'd heard no talk of either of those possibilities. But it made sense that something like that might happen.

Marcus took another gulp. "How old are you?"

"Thirteen."

"Ever tell anyone about that window guard?"

I shook my head.

"Think that had anything to do with Darnell?"

I realized he'd probably never bothered to investigate the window frame in Darnell's room the way I had. Then again, I had only a feeling about who might have kicked out that window guard but no actual proof. "Maybe."

Marcus studied me silently. "You got a lot of sense for your age, DeShawn. More than most cats twice your age. Your momma was that way."

I looked up, surprised. "You knew her?"

Marcus nodded. "She used to babysit me and my brother and sister sometimes."

"You have a brother?"

"Had one."

"How—," I began, and then caught myself. Even at the age of thirteen, I knew he'd probably been shot, OD'd, or maybe died from AIDS.

For a moment Marcus's eyes were soft and sad, and I wondered how many people had ever seen that look from him. Then he got up and took a white envelope from a pair of black pants hanging over the back of a chair. He held the envelope open to me. Inside were bills. I thought I saw a hundred and a fifty. Marcus closed the envelope and sealed it with his tongue.

"Know what bail is, DeShawn?" he asked.

I shook my head.

"Say I get arrested," Marcus said. "My trial may not get scheduled for six months. The police can keep me in jail till then unless I post bail." He handed me the envelope. "This is bail money. If I get arrested, I'll send word about what to do with it."

"You're gonna be arrested?" I asked.

Marcus chuckled. "Sooner or later. If I ain't killed first. You put that in a safe place. Don't tell anyone. Not even your gramma."

"Why me?"

"It can't come from anyone in the Disciples, or the police'll know it's tainted. Gotta come from someone on the outside. Someone I can trust."

I looked down at the envelope, then thought of something and held it back toward him. "What if *you* tell someone? Word gets out I have this money, they'll kill me if I don't give it to them. Probably kill my sister and Gramma, too."

Marcus didn't take the envelope. "You keep it."

"Can't you find someone else?" I asked.

He shook his head slowly. "It's got to be you."

"Why?"

"'Cause you're the only one that don't want it."

RANCE

"Where'd you get that scrawny mutt, Bulb?" Bublz asked out in the yard. We were hanging around the bench. Felt like we'd spent the whole summer there. Bublz was eating Cracker Jacks. He was always eating something.

"Found him," Lightbulb said. The little brown dog tugged at the clothesline leash, mouth open, tongue hanging out. Its ribs showed through the short fur, and its paws looked too big for the rest of him.

"How do you know he don't belong to someone else?" I asked.

"Anyone says he's theirs, I'll give him back," said Lightbulb. "But so far no one's said nothing."

Bublz shoved a handful of Cracker Jacks into his mouth. "He's gonna choke himself if he keeps pulling like that. What's his name?"

"Snoop."

"Snoop Dog," Bublz smirked. "He's too dumb to know he's choking himself."

Lightbulb looked down at his new pet with concern. "He ain't dumb, is he, DeShawn?"

"Nah, just young. He'll learn." I gazed around the yard. "Anyone seen Terrell?"

"You want to go up to his place?" Lightbulb asked. "He can meet Snoop."

"What floor's he on?" Bublz asked.

"Sixth," I said.

Bublz shook his head. "Too far to climb."

Lightbulb and I started toward the building. Snoop squirmed against the leash, sniffing everything. He found an empty Twix wrapper and started to eat it.

"No, Snoop! You don't want that garbage." Lightbulb worked the candy wrapper out of his mouth. The little dog immediately started sniffing around again.

"When's the last time you fed him?" I asked.

"Ain't fed him yet," Lightbulb answered.

"How long have you had him?"

"Since yesterday."

"No wonder he's so hungry."

"Got nothing to feed him," Lightbulb said.

"After we see Terrell, we'll get him something to eat," I said.

Upstairs we knocked on Terrell's door. It had been at least two days since I'd seen him. We could hear the TV on loud.

"Who's there?" Terrell yelled.

"DeShawn and Lightbulb," I answered.

The door opened and Terrell stood there bare chested, wearing pajama bottoms. His eyes looked bleary and bloodshot. "S'up?"

"You been sick?" I asked.

"Who's that?" Mrs. Blake came slapping out of the kitchen.

"Can Terrell come out?" Lightbulb asked.

"No, he can't," Mrs. Blake said. "He's grounded. Can't see no friends, neither. So say good-bye and git."

Lightbulb glanced at Terrell and dropped his voice. "You being punished?" But he didn't drop his voice enough.

"Darn right he is," said Mrs. Blake. "One week in the house for stealin' money outta my purse. And being real sneaky about it too. Five dollars here, ten dollars there, hopin' I wouldn't notice."

Terrell's face colored, and he closed the door. So that was where his big wad of gwap had come from.

Back outside, Lightbulb and I walked down Abernathy. The air was cooler and drier than the day before. Like fall was coming. King Chicken was near Washington Carver Middle School, on the border between Douglass and Gentry. There was a parking lot in the front. In the back, a dented, red Dumpster stood against a wall, and the asphalt around it was littered with paper cups and plates, straws, and other garbage. It smelled like rancid milk and rot, but Snoop started yelping and pawing at the ground, tugging as hard as he could.

"Whoa, Snoop!" Lightbulb gasped. I found a milk crate to stand on and managed to reach into the Dumpster, grab some white paper bags, and toss them

onto the ground. Snoop tore into them and started jaw-
ing on a piece of chicken.

"Guess you were right," Lightbulb said.

The loud squeal of tires made us jump. A black
Range Rover with dark windows and big, glittering
rims screeched around the side of the building and
skidded to a stop. Lightbulb and I ducked behind the
Dumpster. Snoop stayed out in the open, chewing on a
chicken leg. We could hear the bones cracking between
his teeth.

Three men got out of the Range Rover wearing
green and yellow beads around their necks and green
bandanas in their pockets—Gentry Gangstas. I put my
hand on Lightbulb's shoulder and slowly drew him
farther back into the shadows behind the Dumpster to
make sure we wouldn't be seen.

One of the Gangstas was medium height, with broad
shoulders, and wore a baseball cap backward. Reaching
into the car, he yanked out a skinny, old, crusty-looking
man with a scruffy gray beard and dirty, torn ghetto
clothes. He looked like an old hype or wino, and he was
trembling, his yellow eyes wide with fear.

The broad-shouldered Gangsta pushed the old guy
down on his knees before the other two men. One was
narrowly built with dark skin, sharp chiseled features,
and long pointed sideburns. He stood with his arms
crossed and an impassive expression on his face. Like a
judge. The other was just plain big, like a football player,
with a shaved head under a black do-rag. He grabbed the

old guy by the collar and shook him like a floppy doll.

"This is your last chance, Rodney," the big guy threatened. "Tell him!"

"I don't know nothing!" The scruffy guy trembled and sounded like he was going to cry. "I swear!"

The Gangsta with the broad shoulders pulled out a big black gun and stuck it against Rodney's neck. My hand was still on Lightbulb's shoulder, and I felt him shudder. He started to breathe hard and fast. I squeezed his shoulder reassuringly.

"We don't want to kill you," the broad-shouldered one said.

"But I swear," Rodney stammered. "I didn't see nothing. I didn't hear nothing. I don't know nothing. I swear it, Mr. Rance."

I caught my breath. Rance was the leader of the Gentry Gangstas. And that meant the big Gangsta was Big D, the second in command. Rodney's eyes filled with tears, and he intertwined his fingers and pleaded for mercy. Rance stood over him, his arms still crossed, his face blank.

A dozen feet from them, Snoop began to gag. Rance and the other gangbangers glanced at the dog and then back to Rodney.

"This is your last chance, Rodney," Rance said in a slow, deep voice.

"But I don't know nothing!" the old guy wailed. "I swear!"

Crack! The broad-shouldered gangbanger smashed

the butt of the gun hard against Rodney's nose. The old guy clutched his face with his hands, and bright red blood began to seep out between his gnarled fingers. Lightbulb tensed even more. He was breathing so hard, I was afraid he might pass out.

Snoop kept retching and shaking his head as if something was caught in his throat. The gangbangers looked at him again; then Rance kneeled until he was eye level with Rodney and spoke in that calm voice. "You really think this is worth dying for?"

My whole body tensed as I wondered if they'd kill him before our eyes. Again Snoop coughed and gagged like he was choking. At the interruption, Rance turned his head sharply with an annoyed expression. As if taking a cue, the broad-shouldered Gangsta aimed his gun at the little dog.

"*Don't!*" Lightbulb screamed. Before I could stop him, he jumped out from behind the Dumpster and ran to his dog.

Startled, Big D quickly pulled his gun, and both he and the broad-shouldered gangbanger aimed at my friend as he knelt beside the choking dog. Afraid that they might shoot both Lightbulb and Snoop, I stepped from behind the Dumpster.

"What the hell!" Rance grumbled.

Now the Gangstas aimed their guns at me. My heart was racing, and I felt my lungs expanding and contracting as if I'd just sprinted a quarter mile. This was the first time anyone had ever aimed a gun at me. The merest movement of a finger could send pieces of lead ripping through my flesh.

Slowly raising my hands to shoulder height, my eyes met Rance's.

"Anyone else back there?" he asked, almost amused.

I tried to sound calm. "No, sir. Please don't aim those guns at us. We ain't done nothing."

But the guns stayed on Lightbulb and me, as if the gangbangers knew from experience that this was what Rance expected.

"What're you kids doing back here?" Rance asked.

"J-just getting my dog some food," Lightbulb sputtered, hugging Snoop and trembling from head to toe. "Please don't hurt us, please."

Rance's gaze returned to me. He had black tear tattoos beside both eyes. Snoop retched loudly and coughed up some chewed chicken and bones. The little dog began whimpering.

"Get lost," Rance said. Lightbulb picked up Snoop, and we ran all the way home.

HERO

It was the evening before school was supposed to start. Terrell's punishment for stealing was over, and he and I were in his room playing Grand Theft Auto on his Xbox.

"Terrell!" Mrs. Blake suddenly screamed. We raced into the living room. Laqueta was flat on her back on the floor. Her eyes had rolled up into her head and only the whites showed. Terrell's momma was straddling her, slapping her face, and crying, "Come on, baby, wake up! Wake up!" When she saw us she yelled, "Call 911!"

Terrell ran into the kitchen. Mrs. Blake kept slapping Laqueta. White foam trickled from the corner of her mouth. When Terrell came back, his momma said, "Go downstairs and wait for the ambulance. Soon as it gets here, bring the men up."

Terrell and I went down to the yard. It felt like a long time passed before we could hear the sirens. After a while, a boxy, red and white ambulance pulled up to the curb with its lights flashing. The two men inside took their time getting out. One was white, the other black. They looked around warily, as if this project was the last place in the world they wanted to be.

"Come on!" Terrell anxiously pointed back at the building. "My cousin's out cold. We don't know if she's OD'd and passed out or what."

"She drink? Take drugs?" asked the black ambulance man.

"Both," said Terrell.

"Better get the stretcher," the white one said. They went around and opened the back doors, still taking their sweet time. The black ambulance man started to wheel the stretcher toward the building while his partner stayed behind with the truck.

"Maybe you both better come," I said. "Could take two to carry her down."

"Or maybe you got friends in there waiting to jump us," said the white one. "Or we'll get back here, and the ambulance'll be ransacked for drugs and needles. So I'll stay here and keep an eye on the truck."

There was no use arguing. Terrell and I followed the black ambulance man wheeling the stretcher toward the building. He kept looking around as if he expected at any second to get jumped. We went into the lobby, and he pushed the stretcher toward the elevators.

"The elevator's broke," Terrell said, and pointed at the stairwell. "We gotta walk up."

The ambulance man hesitated. "How far?"

"Sixth floor."

The man shook his head. "You'll have to bring her down."

"You crazy?" Terrell began to bluster, but I grabbed his arm to stop him and asked, "How?"

"Make a sling with a blanket," he said. "Four of you can do it if each one holds a corner. Won't take long."

Halfway up the stairs, Terrell started gasping and had to stop and use his inhaler. By the time we got to the apartment, LaRue and Marcus were there. They'd moved Laqueta to the couch, but she was still limp. More foamy spit dripped from the corner of her mouth. Mrs. Blake carefully dabbed it with a towel.

"Where are the ambulance men?" Marcus asked.

"Wouldn't climb up the stairs," I said, and told him about the sling.

Marcus cursed and told Mrs. Blake to find a blanket. When we moved Laqueta, her arms and legs flopped every which way, and her head rolled loosely. Marcus, LaRue, Terrell, and I each picked up a corner. With the four of us lifting her, we went out into the hall and started down the stairs. Marcus and LaRue went first because they were taller and stronger. Even then Terrell and I struggled to hold up our end. Mrs. Blake yelled at us each time we let Laqueta bump against a step.

Pop! Pop! Pop! We were on the fourth floor when the shooting started outside and the sounds of shouting drifted up the stairs.

Marcus momentarily lowered the blanket with Laqueta to the floor, then lifted again. "We gotta get her down. Come on."

The lobby was full of people who'd run inside to get away from the shooting. Most stayed clear of the doors and were huddled near the stairs. We eased Laqueta down on the lobby floor, and once again Mrs. Blake slapped her face, trying to wake her. Snoop trotted by, sniffing here and there. I found Lightbulb hiding under the stairs with his eyes squeezed tight and his fingers in his ears.

I shook his shoulder. "You see an ambulance man?"

Lightbulb opened his eyes. "He left when the shooting started."

Jamar came in from outside with a skinny Disciple named Tyrone, who was grimacing and clutching his arm. Blood darkened his shirt and dripped to the floor. Marcus spoke to them, then he, LaRue, and Jamar went back out through the lobby doors, reaching toward their belts to pull guns.

"Come on," Terrell whispered. He wanted to follow them. I don't know why I went. It was stupid, but in the excitement, I wanted to see. Outside the night air smelled of burned gunpowder. Terrell and I pressed against the building. The bricks still felt warm from being in the sun all day. In the dark the yard looked empty, but slowly I began to see shapes. A woman cradled a baby behind a tree near an overturned baby stroller. Two old men lay on the ground near a bench, covering their heads with their arms.

Pop! Pop! Pop!

Terrell and I ducked down. The shots were coming

from around the corner of the building. Terrell crept to the edge and peeked, then waved for me to join him. I scampered up. Out in the yard, Marcus ducked behind a bench. LaRue crouched behind a metal garbage can.

Pop! Pop! Pop!

They both fired and then moved forward as if driving the invaders back toward Abernathy Avenue. Jamar followed, reaching each spot only after Marcus or LaRue left it.

Pop! Pop! Pop! More shots, then car doors slammed and car tires screeched. There was silence for a moment. Then the normal sounds of a summer evening—car horns, the rumble of bus engines, music, even voices—began to return.

Out in the yard, Jamar rose to his feet. But where were Marcus and LaRue?

People began to come out like rabbits leaving their holes after the fox goes away—slowly and carefully, stopping and listening before taking another step.

There was still no sign of Marcus or LaRue. Suddenly I felt scared. Marcus wasn't just the leader of the Disciples. He was the father none of us had. He gave us jobs, issued orders, settled disputes, and kept people in line. It wasn't until that moment that I realized how people depended on him and needed to know he was there.

Two figures came around the corner. Even in the dark I could see that their clothes were disheveled and their arms hung loosely at their sides. As Marcus passed, he glared at Jamar and spit on the ground. Jamar began to say something, then clammed up and hung his head. We all knew he'd been a coward. Terrell and I followed Marcus back into the building. By now most of the people had left the lobby. A few women were still bent over Laqueta. Someone had rolled up a shawl under her head, and someone else was fanning her with a newspaper while Mrs. Blake dabbed a wet cloth against her forehead.

"DeShawn!" My sister's anxious voice called from the stairwell. "Anyone seen DeShawn?"

"In the lobby," I yelled back.

Nia came to the top of the stairs with her hands on her big belly and consternation on her face. "Gramma wants you upstairs *right now!*"

I could feel people's eyes on me, and wished she didn't sound so bossy. Nia came down the stairs, grabbed me by the arm, and squeezed hard. Suddenly I knew it wasn't just Gramma who wanted me out of harm's way.

Meanwhile Marcus lifted Laqueta in his arms. Her head rolled back. "We'll take my car."

Someone held the door open, and he went through sideways careful not to let his sister bang into the door frame. LaRue, Mrs. Blake, and Terrell followed. Marcus was a gang leader and drug dealer, almost surely a murderer, and as brutal and hard as anyone I'd ever met. But he was the only hero we knew.

JUMPED IN

A few days later I walked home from school with a black cloud over my head. It was Friday and Tanisha wanted us to go to the movies with friends that night, but I had no money and no way to get any. I couldn't decide which was worse: telling Tanisha we couldn't go, or going and letting her pay.

"Hey," someone said.

I looked up. Marcus's black Mercedes was rolling slowly along the curb beside me. He steered with one hand and leaned his elbow out the open window. "What's wrong?"

"Who said anything's wrong?" I said.

"Looks like you got the weight of the world on your shoulders," he said, pulling the car to the curb. "I been drivin' alongside you for almost a whole block, and you ain't looked up once. You got a problem, maybe I can help."

That reminded me of something. "Laqueta okay?"

"Yeah, she's back home now." He gazed at me with steady eyes. "You gonna tell me what's botherin' you?"

"I can take care of it," I said.

If a muscle in Marcus's face moved, I didn't see it. "Come over here. What grade you in?"

"Seventh."

"How you doin'?"

"Okay. I may even go to Hewlett Academy over in Beech Hill." That very day, Mr. Brand had given me a red folder filled with a dozen pages of words he wanted me to learn for the magnet school entrance exam.

"You gotta take some kind of a test to get in?" Marcus asked.

"Yeah. Vocabulary, math, a lot of stuff."

"And suppose you get in," he said. "Then what?"

"I don't know. Get a better education, I guess."

Marcus rubbed his chin across his forearm. "So how come you're mopin' along like your dog just got run over?"

Suddenly I knew I was going to tell him. It was the kind of thing you wanted to talk about with a guy who had experience. "My girl wants to go on a date tonight, and I'm a little short."

"That's messed up," he said, nodding slowly. "How bad do you want to go?"

"I don't care," I said. "But my girl wants to go so bad, she says she'll even pay."

"No way." Marcus shook his head, and I knew he understood. His arm disappeared from the open window. When it reappeared, a bill was folded between his fingers. "Fifty do you?"

I hesitated. "What you want in return?"

"Nothing."

That night Tanisha and I went to the movies with her friends. It was the first time we'd been alone in the dark—the first time I'd been alone in the dark with any girl—and when the movie was over, my life had changed. I was on my way to becoming a man.

Afterward I walked home. Subwoofers boomed from the slow-moving rides cruising the streets, and styled-up folks waited in lines to get into clubs. It was Friday night, and everyone was trying to get what they'd waited for all week.

In the yard at Douglass, people were having a home-coming party for a guy named Derek who'd just gotten out of the army. Dance music blared from a sound system rigged to a car battery. Jamar was talking to a girl with a big chest and short brown hair pasted tightly to her skull. In the shadows near one of the trees, LaRue was slow dancing with a skanky-looking girl in high heels with bleached-blond pigtails and a short, low-cut dress. I pretended not to see him and hoped nobody told Nia.

I was about to go in when I noticed someone on the bench, bent over with his head on his arms. "Terrell?"

My best friend lifted his head. Even in the dark I could see that one of his eyes was swollen shut and dried blood caked his nose and lips.

"What the hell?" I said.

He made a fist. On the back of his hand were three ugly, reddish cigarette burns. Then he pulled a string of black-and-white beads from under his shirt and gave me the sign of the Disciples. A crooked smile worked its way onto his swollen lips. He was in.

FOURTEEN YEARS OLD

When President Bush signed the No Child Left Behind Act in January of 2002, he promised that by 2014 the quality of inner-city school education would catch up to that of suburban schools. But by 2007 the gap between black and white eighth graders was worse than ever.

"STRUGGLE IS MY ADDRESS, WHERE PAIN AND CRACK LIVES,
. . . BORN ON THE BLACK LIST, TOLD I'M BELOW AVERAGE."
—FROM "A DREAM" BY COMMON

23RD PERCENTILE

"I wish we could be alone," Tanisha whispered in my ear. We were in the hall between classes, pressed against her locker, pressed against each other. We were eighth graders now and sought each other out whenever we could.

"Me too." I kissed her. She smelled like cocoa butter, and the mixed sensations of pleasure and yearning were enough to make my knees feel weak. But it was nearly impossible for us to be alone. Lately there'd been more and more shooting between the Disciples and the Gangstas. Anyone, not just gangbangers, from Douglass found in Gentry territory was liable to be shot.

"Maybe you could come over after school," she whispered with closed eyes as I kissed her neck.

Despite the danger, I was seriously tempted.

"My momma'll be at work, and William's never around."

I'd never met her older brother, William, but I knew he was a Gentry Gangsta.

"Let me think about it. . . ." We pressed together,

feeling more heat than the friction of our clothes alone could create.

"Enough of that, you two," someone snapped sharply. It was Ms. Rodriguez, the assistant principal.

I backed slowly away from Tanisha. Past were the days of jumping when some authority figure gave an order.

"I'm getting tired of telling you two to find some place else for that." The old white-haired woman focused on me. "DeShawn, come to my office."

"Sorry, Ms. Rodriguez," I said. "It won't happen again."

"This is about something else," she said.

In her office I sat in an old wooden chair. Ms. Rodriguez pulled a pink sweater over her shoulders. "Now you know why I spend so much time in the halls," she said with a shiver while she searched through a pile of folders on her desk. "Been years since any heat came out of that radiator. Here we are." She opened a folder. "Mr. Brand left instructions for you to take the entrance exam for Hewlett Academy."

"What happened to him, anyway?" I asked. It was November, and I had not yet seen him around school.

"He took a job at one of the suburban schools," Ms. Rodriguez said. "Too bad. He was one of our better teachers."

While the assistant principal studied the folder, I watched through the dirty, bar-covered window as a crusty old bum, who looked like he was wearing three coats, trudged past lugging a huge plastic bag filled with empty cans. "Now, you understand, DeShawn, that we're only allowed to submit a certain number of students for that exam. Have you prepared?"

I shook my head. I'd never gotten around to studying the list of words Mr. Brand had given me.

Mrs. Rodriguez frowned. "Let's take a look at your transcript anyway." She turned to her computer and studied the screen, tapping a bony finger against her lower lip. "You are certainly one of the better students, especially among the boys."

"Mr. Brand said I was reading at grade level," I said proudly.

"Let's see your standardized test results." She typed and a different screen appeared on the computer. Her eyebrows dipped. "City-wide, your test scores are in the twenty-third percentile."

"What's that mean?" I asked, although I could tell by her expression that it wasn't good.

"Compared to students from all the other schools, you're in the bottom quarter."

The radiator made a faint gurgling sound, as if water was struggling to get through.

"It's not your fault, DeShawn," Ms. Rodriguez said. "Many children get private tutoring or special preparation for these entrance exams. Things we can't give students here."

Secretly, I felt relief. I didn't want to leave Tanisha and take a bus every day to Beech Hill. And now I didn't have to feel bad about letting Mr. Brand down, because he could have come back to Washington Carver if he'd really cared.

Ms. Rodriguez tapped the bottom of the folder against the desk. "All right?" She had other things to do. I got up and started to leave.

"DeShawn?" she said. "One other thing. Your friend Raydale Diggs."

"Who?"

"I believe you call him Lightbulb?"

It had been so long since I had heard his real name, I'd forgotten it.

"Maybe you could do us a favor," Ms. Rodriguez said. "He's one of the brightest children we've ever seen here, and we would like him to apply to Hewlett Academy, but he seems reluctant. Perhaps you'd talk to him? You're a friend, so he might listen to you."

DEALER

Nia had twins—a boy named Xavier and a girl named Jayda—and the population in our apartment increased by three, not two, because LaRue moved in. Gramma gave her bedroom to the new family. Now she slept on the couch, and I slept on the floor on a small mattress that we hid behind the curtains during the day. In no time it felt like those babies took over the whole apartment. The kitchen counter was covered with plastic baby bottles and cans of baby formula, and the garbage can was a heap of stinky Pampers. Hand-washed baby clothes and maternity bras hung in the bathroom. I spent as much time as I could outside.

Terrell and I were hanging around the bench talking to Precious and listening to 50 Cent on Terrell's boom box. He was wearing his black Disciples colors, his cap turned to the right, and his sleeves rolled up to show off his new tattoos. Precious wore a lot of eye makeup, and her fingernails were long and painted blue. Her tight, white T-shirt said SO MANY BOYZ, SO LITTLE TIME.

The material was so thin that you could see the pink bra underneath.

"Your daddy see you dress like that?" Terrell asked.

Precious's face hardened. "He ain't around no more." When she talked, you saw the stud in her tongue.

"What happened?" Terrell asked.

"What do you *think* happened?" she shot back, as if it were obvious. She glanced at the boom box balanced on Terrell's knees. "Why you got that hunk of junk? Can't you afford an iPod?"

"What's the point?" Terrell asked, slightly annoyed.

"Get a lot more songs than those cheap bootleg CDs you play." Precious spoke in a taunting, angry way, as if challenging his manhood. So different from that cute little girl in the pink jacket a few years back who was so proud that her daddy lived with her.

Terrell played it slow and cool, like he had nothing to prove. "Trouble with that iPod is you can't listen with your peeps," he said, gesturing toward me. But the truth was, putting music on an iPod required a computer, and neither Terrell nor I had one.

"Want to go out sometime?" Terrell asked her.

"With who?" Precious asked haughtily, and pretended to look around for someone worthy of her.

"Who do you think?" Terrell asked.

She gave him a cool appraisal. "You? You ain't nothing but a two-bit crack dealer. Where we gonna go? You got money? You got a car? You even old enough to drive? 'Cause I ain't going on no bus date."

"I can get a car if I want," Terrell said.

"Uh-huh. Sure you can."

A hype came up, all ashy skin and bones, missing teeth and wearing filthy, ragged clothes. We called them "the walking dead." She handed Terrell some money, and he pointed at a shorty leaning against a wall, head bent, thumbs flying over the controls of a PSP. The kid couldn't have been more than nine years old. He led the hype inside the building.

Dealers used shorties to hold their crack, weed, and pills because the worst thing the cops could do was confiscate the drugs and take the kid home to his momma. Everyone knew the courts wouldn't put eight- and nine-year olds in juvie for drugs. The mothers knew it too. Some of them waited until the cops left and then sent their kids back out to work.

"So maybe you got some money," Precious said, but what she didn't know was that almost every penny Terrell earned went to the Disciples, not Terrell. She took a compact out of her bag and checked her make-up.

Terrell cleared his throat. "So? Wanna go out?"

Precious gazed up over the compact at him. "You better have a car, and you better take me some place nice." She snapped the compact shut, spun on her toes, and walked away.

Terrell grinned and held out his palm for me to slap. "Friday night's starting to look good."

The day drifted past. I hung around the bench with Terrell. Girls played jump rope. Young mothers pushed babies in strollers, and old folks hobbled past on canes. No one else came by for drugs, and after a while Terrell's shorty said he had to go.

Then Bublz showed up. "Look what I got." He fanned out a bunch of King Chicken coupons. "Buy one, get one free."

I was hungry. Most of the food stamps and welfare money that month had gone toward baby formula and Pampers. Terrell hadn't left the bench in hours. He had to be hungry too.

"Can't," said Terrell.

Bublz looked around. "Come on. You'll be back in twenty minutes. No one'll know you was gone."

On the way to King Chicken we ran into Lightbulb being pulled by Snoop, who'd grown to be a medium-size dog but was still as wild as a pup.

"You gotta train that dog, Bulb," Terrell said.

"He's trained," Lightbulb insisted.

"Hey," I said. "Ms. Rodriguez wants to know why you won't apply for that Hewlett Acdemy."

"My momma can't pay for no bus," Lightbulb said.

"Maybe Bulb ain't smart enough," Terrell said.

"Ms. Rodriguez says he's one of the smartest they've ever seen."

"Him?" Terrell pointed at our friend. "No way."

Lightbulb hung his head.

"You guys go ahead," I said to Terrell and Bublz. "I'll catch up."

When they were out of earshot, Lightbulb scuffed his foot against the ground. "I don't want to go, DeShawn. Just want to stay where I am."

"But this is nowhere."

Lines appeared in his brow. "I'm happy here."

"For now. But then what? You gonna be a gang-banger?"

Lightbulb shook his head. "No. What are *you* gonna do?"

I didn't answer because I didn't know. We watched the cars pass on Abernathy. All those people with places to go.

And we had nowhere to go.

Snoop started to tug on the leash again. "See you," Lightbulb said, and let Snoop drag him away.

A few minutes later I joined Terrell and Bublz in a booth at King Chicken. They were working through a bucket of legs and breasts and slurping from big cups of soda.

"I'm takin' out Precious Friday night," Terrell announced.

"I thought she only dates older guys," said Bublz.

Terrell grinned. "Older guys . . . and me."

"She said you had to drive," I reminded him.

"I'll get a car," Terrell replied, as if it were as easy as buying a candy bar. "Jamar showed me how."

"Just because you learned how to steal one doesn't mean you know how to drive one," I said.

"How hard could it be?" Terrell waved at the traffic outside. "Look at those dumb asses driving around."

The door to King Chicken swung open, and Marcus marched in. Terrell and Bublz had their backs to the door and didn't see him. But Terrell must've seen it in my face because he started to turn around.

Wham! Marcus smacked him on the side of the head. In the next booth a lady with two small kids screamed. Bublz cowered in the corner of the booth, his eyes squeezed shut and his arms covering his head. I jumped up, my lap dark with spilled soda. Terrell was too stunned by the blow to move.

Wham! Marcus smacked him again. Everyone in King Chicken stopped eating. Some people hurried for the door. Terrell huddled against Bublz, who was still cowering in the corner. Marcus raised his open hand again. "I say you could leave that bench?"

"Wasn't nothing happening," Terrell stammered.

Marcus grabbed him by the collar and yanked him up with one hand until they were practically nose to nose. "You don't decide that, understand? You don't decide nothing. You just do what I tell you."

"I'm telling you," Terrell said in a quavering voice. "Wasn't no one buying nothing."

Marcus flinched and glanced around. He grabbed Terrell by the hair and hauled him out of the booth.

"Ow! Ow! Man, stop it!" Terrell wailed as Marcus

dragged him out of King Chicken. "Ow! Let go, man, I'll go! I'll go!"

But Marcus didn't let go. He dragged Terrell into the parking lot. I followed, keeping my distance. Bublz took off down the sidewalk as fast as his big, bouncing gut would allow. Still holding Terrell by the hair, Marcus backed him against the wall.

"Mistake number one," Marcus growled in a low, ominous voice. "You don't leave that bench unless I tell you to. Ever. Understand?"

Terrell stared at the ground, unwilling to look the gang leader in the eye. Marcus yanked his head up until they were eyeball to eyeball. Terrell's were wet with tears. "I understand," he sniffed.

"Mistake number two," Marcus continued. "You don't talk business when anyone else can hear. Understand?"

Terrell nodded, blinking rapidly. Tears ran down his cheeks. He started to wheeze and quickly dug out his inhaler. Marcus let him go but held his hand close to Terrell's face. My friend winced as if expecting another blow. But instead, Marcus patted his cheek.

"Hey," he said gently. "Everybody makes a mistake."

Terrell looked up at him with reddened eyes and sniffed. "It ain't fair. I sit all day on that bench. Most days I don't even sell fifty dollars worth of rock. Then I got to give all the money to you. I'd make more working here." He nodded toward King Chicken.

"I told you it takes time," Marcus said. "You gotta work your way up. Pay your dues. A year from now you'll be making more in a day than you could make at this place in a month."

Terrell nodded and wiped his eyes with the back of his hand. Marcus looked at me. "Both of you in the car."

Being a Disciple, Terrell rode in the front while I sat in the back. Back at Douglass, Marcus parked on Abernathy and turned to Terrell. "Do your job. And don't let me ever see you leave that bench again."

Terrell got out. I slid across the backseat to get out too, but Marcus looked over the seat at me. "Hold on."

I stopped.

"How's them little babies doing?" he asked.

"Okay."

"LaRue move in?"

I nodded.

"Must be getting kind of crowded in there."

"Uh-huh."

"Ever think that someday you could have a place of your own?" he said. "A place to bring that cute girlfriend of yours."

Tanisha had spent enough time around Douglass for just about everyone to know she was my girl, but it still surprised me that Marcus paid attention to things like that. I glanced out the window at Terrell, who'd gotten back up on the bench.

"That won't be you," Marcus said.

I swiveled my head toward him. "How come?"

"Still got that envelope I gave you?"

"Uh-huh."

"Ever tell anyone?"

I shook my head.

"See, DeShawn, the Disciples is like a company," Marcus said. "Different guys get different jobs. All depends on what the boss thinks you're good for. Right now Terrell's on that bench because that's what he's good for. You'd be good for other things. Things that pay a lot better."

I gazed at the teardrop tattoo at the corner of his eye. Maybe I should have been afraid, but I wasn't. I'd noticed something about Marcus. He could get really mad when you did something wrong, but he also listened when you spoke your mind. "I think you forgot to tell Terrell that there's a chance in a year he'll be making good money, but there's a better chance that he'll be dead or in jail."

"He knows that," said Marcus. "He'd have to be stupid not to."

It got quiet in the car as if Marcus was thinking. Then he said, "Listen, DeShawn, you don't have to worry about being jumped in. You'll get blessed in. No one'll touch you."

I tried to hide my surprise that he was so eager for me to join the Disciples. Marcus leaned closer. "You're a smart kid. Not school smart; street smart. It ain't something they give grades for. It's just something you're born with."

"Something I got from my momma?"

"That's right."

"If she was so smart, how come she's dead?"

Marcus gazed at me thoughtfully with his small, deep-set eyes. "Bad luck. She was in the wrong place at the wrong time. Could have been anyone."

"Not me," I said.

"Even you." He gazed past me and suddenly his face hardened. I turned and saw that Officer Patterson had pulled to the curb behind us in his police cruiser. Marcus tilted his head toward the door. I got out and he drove away, but Officer Patterson didn't. He just sat in his car, watching me.

WILLIAM

Rain swept down in sheets. Tanisha and I pulled our hoodies up and jogged along the sidewalk, sometimes ducking into doorways when the downpour got too hard.

We were in the Gentry Project where the buildings weren't tall like at Douglass. They were newer and mostly four stories, set in circles with walkways like spokes meeting in a central courtyard. On the outside they looked nicer, but in the lobby of Tanisha's building the mailboxes were smashed just like the ones in my building. Tanisha pulled back her dripping hood and shook out her hair. I wanted to pull off my wet hood too, but I didn't dare.

Her apartment was dark and quiet. Instead of a sheet and blanket, the couch in the living room was covered with clear plastic. Tanisha led me down the hall and into her room. The bed had a flowery pink and white cover and some stuffed animals. A big poster of Will Smith hung on the wall along with sketches of women in dresses and skirts. Tanisha wanted to be a fashion designer, and there were sketch pads on the floor beside neat piles of fashion magazines. On the small makeup table were bottles of perfume and makeup and a small radio/CD player.

She sat on the bed and pulled me down next to her, then leaned her head on my shoulder. For a while we just sat with our legs hanging over the edge, catching our breath after running. The idea that I was in Gentry territory, in the home of an actual Gentry Gangsta, was stuck in my head, making me tense and uncomfortable.

Tanisha pulled off her hoodie. "You gonna take off yours?" she asked, teasing.

"Oh, yeah." I pulled it over my head and let it fall to the floor. Tanisha kissed my neck and then my ear, but I was having a hard time relaxing.

She backed off. "What's wrong?"

"Sorry, Tani. It's just being here."

"My momma won't be home for at least an hour and a half."

"And your brother?"

"I *told* you. He's never home." She leaned close and started to kiss my neck and ears again, and slowly tingling promises of pleasure took over.

Bang! A door closed hard. I sat up straight and exchanged a wide-eyed look with Tanisha.

"It must be him," she gasped.

My heart began hammering.

She squeezed my hand. "Maybe he'll go."

Maybe . . . or maybe not. Meanwhile I was trapped in Tanisha's bedroom. The window had bars across it. If I got caught under her bed, I'd be defenseless. I rose and stood by the closet, ready to disappear inside.

From the kitchen came the sound of the refrigerator door opening and closing. The TV went on.

"Doesn't sound like he's leaving," I whispered.

Tanisha bit her lip and looked at the clock on her night table. "Momma's gonna be home in an hour."

"What are we gonna do?" I asked.

"You gotta sneak out," Tanisha said. "I'll unlock the front door, then go talk to William. You wait here. When I ask him if it's supposed to keep raining, that means the coast is clear. You tiptoe down the hall and let yourself out. Okay?"

I don't know why we smiled at each other, but we did. Tanisha kissed me quickly and left the room. I pulled my damp hoodie back on and stood in the doorway, listening. But the TV was loud, and it was hard to tell whether I was hearing Tanisha and William, or the people on the TV.

I stepped quietly into the hall. The living room was on the left, and I stopped just before it and listened again. Now all I heard was the TV. Then Tanisha said loudly, "So is it gonna keep raining or not?"

"What are you hollering for?" an annoyed male voice asked. "And why're you asking me that when you just asked me a minute ago? What're you looking at anyway?"

"Nothing!" Tanisha answered with a frightened gasp.

I heard shifting sounds and plastic squeak as if someone had just risen from the couch.

"You don't have to get up!" Tanisha protested.

Her brother's answer came in footsteps. Out in the hall, I considered dashing back into Tanisha's room, but there wasn't time. Instead I raised my hands to shoulder height so that William would see that I wasn't carrying. He stepped out into the hall and started when he saw me. He was wearing a green jersey and black, baggy jeans. I didn't get a good look at his face. I was too busy watching his hand reach toward his belt.

Tanisha rushed into the hall behind him. "William! Don't!"

Her brother pulled a black gun from his waist and pointed it at me. My heart was beating so hard that I began to feel light-headed and had to remind myself to breathe. "Who are you?" William demanded.

"He's a friend of mine." Tanisha stepped next to me.

"How the hell'd you get in here?" her brother asked.

I couldn't take my eyes off that gun. At any second it might go off. Even if it was an accident, it wouldn't matter.

"I let him in," Tanisha said.

"The hell you did," William said. "You were in the living room bothering me about the weather."

"No, I meant *before* you came home," Tanisha quickly explained.

Her brother lowered the gun. As the barrel went down, my eyes went up, past the string of green and yellow beads, to his face. He was broad-shouldered, and I knew I'd seen him before, but it took a second to remember where. That day behind King Chicken with Lightbulb and Snoop. William was the one who'd hit the old guy in the face with the butt of his gun and nearly shot Snoop.

I saw a glimmer in William's eye and quickly looked away, but it was too late. "I know you?" he asked.

Staring at the floor, I shook my head.

"Yeah, I do," William said. "I seen you before." He turned to Tanisha. "Where's he from?"

"School," Tanisha answered.

"Yeah, but where's he *from*?"

We both knew what he meant. I didn't want Tanisha to have to say it, so I did. "Douglass."

William cursed and started to raise the gun again.

"He ain't no Disciple!" Tanisha gasped.

"You think it matters?" her brother replied coldly, and glared at me. "How old are you?"

"Fourteen."

"Know any Disciples?"

I nodded. It would have been stupid to lie. You couldn't live in Douglass and not know someone from the gang. By now the gun was level with my eyes.

"You can't shoot him!" Tanisha cried.

"Not here," her brother answered ominously. Keeping the gun on me, he glanced at his sister. "How stupid can you be? What do you think would happen if word got out you was seeing some boy from Douglass?" William swung his head back and forth in disbelief. "Might as well line me up in front of a firing squad."

"Please let him go," Tanisha begged.

"You ever gonna see him again?" William asked.

The question caught us both by surprise. Tanisha's mouth fell open, but no words came out.

"Well?" William demanded.

Tanisha's eyes began to glitter. "But . . . ," she said beseechingly.

"Don't 'but' me," her brother snapped. "Everyone makes mistakes. Now say it before I put a cap between this punk's eyes."

A tear rolled down Tanisha's cheek. She hung her head. "I won't."

"Won't what?"

"Won't see him again." Tanisha let out an anguished cry and ran into the living room. Even with the TV on, we could hear her sobbing.

William aimed the gun at me. "When you go, keep your head down. Don't let anyone get a good look at you. Go straight back to Douglass. And so help me, I ever see you on this side of town again . . . I ever *hear* that you came near my sister again, I will hunt you down and kill you sure as the sun will rise."

DICE

Nia banged on the bathroom door. "Open up, DeShawn."

"Just a second." The lock was broken, so I kept my foot jammed against the bottom of the door.

"I'm gonna tell Gramma what you're doing," Nia threatened.

"Go ahead." The truth was, I was shaving my upper lip. I didn't have any hair growing there yet, but I'd heard if you shaved, it made your 'stache grow in faster.

Nia banged again. "Come on! I gotta go!"

"Another second." I rinsed the razor and put it back in the medicine cabinet, then wiped my face with a towel to get rid of any telltale shaving cream.

When I opened the door, Nia looked around suspiciously and took a deep sniff. "What're you up to?"

"Nothing," I said with a smile.

Nia squinted her eyes severely, as if accepting a challenge. After grabbing the towel off the rack and burying her face in it, she looked up, puzzled at first, and then frowned. "Shaving cream?"

I felt my face turn hot.

My sister's disapproval turned into a triumphant

smile. "You even got anything to shave, baby face?"

"A little."

"Well, keep your fingers crossed, and maybe you'll be shaving by the time you're twenty-one," she said. "Now get out of here and let me do my business."

I left the bathroom. The bedroom door was open. It was one of those rare, quiet moments when both babies were asleep. LaRue was sitting on the corner of the bed with a small paintbrush in his hand. Curious, I stepped closer and saw that he'd placed half a dozen little jars of paint on the floor and was carefully painting an action figure holding a sword.

"What is it?" I whispered, not wanting to wake the babies sleeping on the bed.

"Warhammer," he answered and pointed at a small, black plastic case, which lay open by his feet. Inside, a dozen painted figures of knights with shields, swords, and spears were nestled in gray foam.

"You painted all of them?" I asked.

LaRue nodded. "I play over at the hobby center."

"Play?"

"It's a strategy game. We have armies that fight each other."

Like gangbangers, I thought, and headed into the living room. Gramma was watching *Judge Joe Brown*, and I knew better than to interrupt her. Her gray hair stuck out unevenly, and she had bags under her eyes. Lately it seemed like she was going to work less and spending more time sitting on that old couch. It used to be that she'd dress up and go out on the weekends more, too. But now she was forty-five, and that was old.

She didn't bother to ask where I was going when I left.

Down in the lobby, Terrell was sitting on an old car seat some guys had dragged inside, drinking a bottle of malt liquor. His mustache was growing in—not enough to shave yet, but what there was made him look older. He wore a chain around his neck and a black leather wristband. Offering the bottle to me, he said, "Wanna play some C-Low?"

Ever since that day at King Chicken when Marcus had slapped him around, Terrell had been changing, forcing himself to get tougher and meaner. He always had gambling and drinking money now. Not what guys called "real" money, like enough to buy a car or even a flat-screen TV. But enough to make life a little more interesting than before.

"Who're you shooting with?" I asked.

"Bublz and some friend of his."

The words were hardly out of his mouth when Bublz and a stocky, ominous-looking guy came into the lobby. The stranger was wearing a black knit cap, a heavy, green and blue plaid shirt, and had an earring.

"This is my cousin Jules," said Bublz proudly, as if he was glad to be related to someone who looked so tough. Unlike the rest of us, Bublz's voice hadn't started to drop yet. He was like a big, chubby, overgrown baby.

"Where you from?" Terrell asked in his "hard" voice, not getting up or offering to shake hands.

"Here, now," Jules answered just as hard and cracked his knuckles. "Just moved in."

"Like it?" Terrell asked, joking.

But Jules didn't get the joke. "You serious? It's worse than ghetto." He looked around impatiently as if he wasn't interested in chitchat. It was all part of the pose. "So, where you want to play?"

"In the back," said Terrell, slowly hoisting himself to his feet, trying to look as menacing as he could. We went down a hall and through a back door. An outside security light provided illumination. A couple of kids were spraying tags on the wall, but now that Terrell was a Disciple, all he had to say was "get lost," and they scattered.

Terrell, Bublz, and Jules knelt down and started to roll. Terrell and Jules were quiet and intense, working hard to out pose each other, while Bublz jabbered nervously in that high voice. Having no gwap to gamble, I stared out into the dark and smoked some bud. The more I smoked and drank, the less sharp and jagged was the pain of missing Tanisha.

I closed my eyes and let my head tilt back. Every sound around me seemed amplified: the clickity clack of the green and red dice, the hopeful mutterings of the guys, followed by disappointed grunts or triumphant chortles, the traffic out on Abernathy, the angry couple yelling from a window somewhere above. It all came together in the music of the projects.

Back in the day when Terrell and I were shorties, there'd been different music in our ears. Playing box ball, cops and robbers, tag, and hide-and-seek, the music was a chorus of laughter and shouting. There were gangs and shootings back then, too. But they were just brief interruptions in the fun and didn't mean anything.

Crash! Smashing glass snapped me back. Jules had tossed a bottle into the dark. "I'm sick of playing for a dollar or two," he grumbled in a voice that sounded syrupy from drink and weed. "Who wants to make it five and ten?"

Terrell's eyes were glazed, and his movements were slow, but there was no way he was backing down. "Sure. Five and ten."

"I don't know," Bublz said nervously. "I ain't got that much."

"Then just watch," Jules grumbled.

Bublz backed away while Jules and Terrell rolled. Soon there was close to eighty dollars lying on the ground, and Jules was shaking the dice. He had to roll a six. The dice skipped across the asphalt and ricocheted off the brick wall. I could have sworn he'd rolled a three, but an instant later his hand swept down, scattering the dice.

"I won," he said, scooping up the bills.

"You rolled a three," said Terrell.

"A six," Jules insisted. Shoving the money into his pocket, he got to his feet and stumbled backward, waving his arms to keep his balance.

"A three." Terrell also rose unsteadily. "Then you knocked the dice away."

They glared at each other. I got up, feeling woozy but alert to the growing sense of danger. The music of the night faded away.

"Where you going anyway?" Terrell asked.

"Gotta fade," Jules said.

"The hell you do," Terrell snarled.

"Hey—," Bublz started to say, but Jules cut him short with, "Shut up." Then Jules glared at Terrell and cracked his knuckles. "Who's gonna stop me?"

"Give me that money," Terrell said.

Jules turned to Bublz. "You tell him. It was a six, right?"

Bublz's eyes darted frantically between his cousin and his friend. He lowered his gaze. "I didn't see."

"Did you see?" Terrell asked me.

I nodded. "Looked like a three."

"Well, you're wrong. It was a six," Jules said, puffing out his chest. "And I gotta bounce." He turned to leave.

"You ain't going nowhere," Terrell threatened. Suddenly he started to wheeze and reached into his Starter jacket for the inhaler.

Jules watched him inhale his medicine, then grinned. "Some tough guy."

Terrell slid his hand inside the Starter jacket again. But this time it didn't come out. "Give back the money, or else."

I felt a chill. Jules stared at the spot where Terrell's hand disappeared into his jacket. His lips parted into a grin. "Or what? You gonna shoot me with your inhaler?"

Terrell took something different out of his pocket—a small, black pistol.

"Oh, no," Bublz whimpered and backed away. Jules stared at the gun, and a taunting smile slowly appeared on his lips. "You ain't got the guts."

"Give the money back," Terrell said coldly. He was trying to act tough and doing a pretty good job of it. Someone who didn't know him as well as I did might think it was real. Or maybe I no longer knew him as well as I thought.

"Give it back, Jules," Bublz warned in a trembling voice. "He's a Disciple,"

"I don't care if he's the NBA, FBI, and NFL," Jules spit.

"You will when you sober up," said Bublz.

Jules ignored his cousin. "He don't have the guts. Probably don't even know how to use that thing. I bet it ain't even loaded."

"This is the last time I'm gonna say it," Terrell warned. "Give me that money."

Jules cursed him.

Terrell lowered the gun. *Bang!*

Bublz and I jumped. Jules went down with a thud and grabbed for his foot. "My foot!" he cried. "He shot my foot!"

"You're lucky I didn't shoot your face," Terrell growled.

Jules lay on the ground, clutching his foot and grimacing. Tears squeezed out of the corners of his eyes. His white sneaker turned red. Bublz stood frozen with his mouth agape and his eyes bulging. Terrell bent over Jules and started going through his pockets, searching for the money.

Wham! Jules swung his arm out hard, catching Terrell square in the face. My friend fell back, and the pistol clattered to the ground about five feet away. Jules rose to his hands and knees. He looked at the gun; then he looked at me.

I knew what he was thinking.

He lunged for the gun. For a kid who'd just been shot in the foot, he moved pretty fast.

But I was faster, scooping up the gun and aiming it down at him. This was the first time I'd ever held a real gun, and even though it was small, it weighed more than I'd expected. My heart was hammering and my hand trembled, but I willed it to stop.

Still on his hands and knees, Jules looked up at me uncertainly. Then, out of nowhere, a different sensation took hold. With that gun in my hand, I began to feel powerful in a way I'd never felt before.

Terrell rose unsteady to his feet and staggered toward me with his hand out. "Gimme."

"No," I said, knowing what would happen if I did.

"I said, gimme!" Terrell demanded.

Keeping Jules in the corner of my eye, I swung my arm around and aimed the gun at Terrell.

"What?" My friend's mouth fell open, and his face scrunched up like he didn't understand. "You . . . " He squinted his eyes. "Whose side you on?"

"Yours, stupid."

Terrell cursed. But it was all for show. I aimed the gun at Jules. "Keep your hands where I can see them. Bublz, take forty dollars out of his pocket and give it to Terrell."

Since Terrell and Jules had been playing head on, half the eighty dollars belonged to each of them. Now they were even.

Terrell counted the bills and shoved them into his pocket. Then he turned to Jules. "I ever see you around here again, I'll kill you soon as look at you." He disappeared into the building.

Jules sat up, holding his foot and moaning. His sneaker and hands were smeared red. Bublz squatted next to him.

"Take him to the emergency room," I said. "Tell them you and him were playing around with a gun, and it went off accidentally."

I bent down in front of Jules. "Know what happens to snitches?"

He didn't respond.

Slap! I smacked him half-hard in the face. "Answer me."

Jules jerked up his head, gritting his teeth venomously. "I know."

"They're gonna try to get you to change your story," I told Bublz, "but no matter what they say, you stick to it. You tell anyone what really happened and—"

"Don't have to tell me." Bublz helped his cousin up. Jules grimaced and draped his arm over Bublz's shoulder for support. He kept the wounded foot raised and hopped on the other foot. But he narrowed his eyes and gave me a look to let me know that if I weren't holding that gun, he'd kill me with his bare hands. A lot of guys may act tough, but if they're shot in the foot and still give a look like that, they *are* tough.

I waited until they left, then went out to the street and threw the gun down a storm drain.

The next day I woke up with a headache. Didn't feel like going to school. I was loafing around watching TV when LaRue came out of the bedroom, buckling his belt. "Get dressed," he said.

I didn't have to ask why. A little while later I was on the fifteenth floor for the first time since that day, two years before, when Marcus gave me his bail money. In the middle of a filthy room, Jules was kneeling with his hands bound behind him and his eyes blindfolded. His lower lip was swollen and split, and his nose was caked with blood. His left foot was wrapped in a bandage, so I knew he'd made it to the emergency room the night before.

Marcus and Terrell were there, along with Tyrone.

"Where's the gun?" Marcus asked me.

"Threw it down a storm drain," I said.

"*What?*" Terrell sputtered.

Marcus gave him a silencing look, then turned to me. "Smart. Cops can't prove nothin' without a weapon." He gestured at Jules. "He cheat?"

I glanced at the blindfolded, cowering figure. "He's new around here and made a mistake. We were all pretty wasted."

"Say *what?*" Terrell gasped incredulously.

With the blindfold on, Jules couldn't see me press my finger against my lips to hush Terrell.

"So you don't think we should kill him?" Marcus asked with a wink.

Jules shuddered.

"Hell, no," I said. "In fact, I think he'd make a pretty good Disciple."

"Over my dead body," Terrell snorted.

"Don't say that," LaRue muttered. "Unless you want it to come true."

FIFTEEN YEARS OLD

In the inner cities it is not uncommon to find twelve-year-olds who cannot read. In some gang-infested neighborhoods in California, only one in twenty high school students can do grade-level math or English.

"HIS LAST WORDS, PROMISE ME THIS MUCH IN DEATH
DON'T LET MY BOY LIVE TO RETRACE MY STEPS."
—FROM "GROWN MAN BUSINESS" BY MOS DEF

BABY DADDY

"DeShawn, wake up." Someone was shaking my shoulder. I opened my eyes. In the dim light, LaRue crouched over me. His long braids were bunched behind his head, held with a band.

"S'up?" I yawned, rising to my elbows from my small mattress on the living room floor. Gramma lay under her blanket on the couch, her mouth open, snoring.

"Something's going on." He pulled back the heavy green curtains. It was a wet March day, and a fine mist hung in the air. Parked along Abernathy Avenue were white vans with NEWS 8 and EYEWITNESS NEWS on their sides. Down in the yard, camera crews and reporters were interviewing people.

"What is it?" I asked, pulling on some clothes.

"Don't know but it must be big," said LaRue.

On the couch, Gramma made a snorting noise and rolled over without opening her eyes. Nia came out of the bedroom with one baby on each hip, both of them sucking their thumbs. "You goin' out?" she asked LaRue. Lately she almost always sounded annoyed with him.

"Maybe."

"Then maybe you won't forget the Pampers this time."

LaRue pulled on his jacket and didn't answer. The more Nia nagged, the quieter he grew. She was always complaining that LaRue didn't help enough and that she never had time to do anything for herself or see her friends. LaRue went to the door, and I followed.

"You better not come back without those Pampers," my sister warned.

Down in the lobby, Terrell, Tyrone, and Marcus were talking in a corner by the broken elevator. Marcus waved LaRue over while I continued outside. Despite the cold, wet mist that left a silvery sheen on everyone's clothes and hair, there were a lot of people out in the yard, mostly around the television cameras with their bright lights and well-dressed reporters.

I ran into Precious, who kept a red umbrella over her head with one hand while she held her jacket closed with the other. She couldn't zip the jacket because her belly stuck out too far. She'd been telling people it was Terrell's baby.

"What's going on?" I asked.

"Two shorties from Number Two shot a pregnant lady. They took her to the hospital. People say she'll probably live, but the baby's dead for sure."

So that explained the news crews. They were asking people if they knew the shorties or the lady who got shot. Most of the people who said they did probably didn't. They just wanted to be on TV. Terrell and LaRue came through the crowd.

"Gotta bounce," LaRue said. He'd been promoted to runner. It was his job to deliver the money and pick up the drugs that souljas like Terrell sold on the street. In some ways it was the most dangerous job in the gang, because much of the time he was either carrying a lot of money or a lot of drugs.

"What about the you-know-whats?" I said, careful not to embarrass him by mentioning the Pampers.

LaRue reached into his pocket and pulled out some bills. "Ain't got time. Do me a favor, okay?"

He took off, leaving Terrell, Precious, and me. Precious gave Terrell a yearning glance. Now that she was going to have his baby, she wasn't so haughty anymore. Other guys weren't interested in pregnant girls.

"Want to do something?" she asked Terrell.

Terrell gave her a cold look. "No."

Precious pursed her lips and almost looked like she was going to cry, but then she set her jaw hard and walked away. Meanwhile Terrell turned to me. "S'up?"

"Gotta go to the store," I said.

Terrell said he'd go with me, and we started walking through the chilly mist.

"Sure it ain't your kid?" I asked.

"No, but I ain't sure it is, either," Terrell said.

"Why would she say it was if it wasn't?"

"'Cause maybe that skank don't know," Terrell said. "Maybe she just thinks I'm the best choice."

"Girls usually know."

"Oh, yeah? Who made you the expert?"

"What if it really is yours?" I asked.

Terrell gave me a disdainful look. "She can't prove it, okay? And I ain't with her no more. Maybe I like Imani better."

Imani was a short, slight girl with long, wavy brown hair. She was soft-spoken and shy, almost the opposite of Precious.

"Since when?" I asked.

"Since whenever," Terrell said, then smiled sheepishly. "And maybe if I'm any baby's daddy, it's hers."

"She's pregnant, too?" I asked.

"Uh-huh." Terrell nodded and grinned. You could see he was proud.

ANIMALS

That night, the shooting of the pregnant woman was the first story on all the news shows. They said doctors had operated to remove the dead baby, and the mother was expected to recover. They didn't show photographs of the nine- and ten-year-old shorties who'd shot her, but they did show an old photo of the victim, and we all agreed that we'd seen her around. The part Gramma and Nia liked the best was when they interviewed our neighbors about what had happened. They'd interview one person, but crowds of others would be around them, all trying to get their faces on TV. It was strangely exciting to see everyday people like us on the same screen that showed the most famous stars and rappers and athletes on earth.

But the fun didn't last. Next the mayor came on and spoke about the shooting as a tragedy, and how not one, but three lives had been destroyed—the woman's unborn child, and the two boys as well. He asked what kind of world it was where children shot mothers-to-be.

The camera moved to an important-looking police

commander standing next to the mayor. He said they were investigating rumors that the boys were part of the Douglass Disciples.

"That's a damn lie," LaRue spat. "I never saw those shorties before."

The camera went back to the mayor, who promised there'd be more police enforcement around Frederick Douglass. Then some commercials came on.

"Good," said Gramma. "Now go back to *Cosby*."

"No," I said, getting up.

Everyone looked surprised. Usually I was the last person to make a fuss about what was on the TV. I turned to a show where three women in dresses and two men in suits were sitting around a table discussing the shooting.

"Ain't we heard enough of this?" Gramma complained.

"Just a little more," I said.

One of the women and one of the men was dark skinned. The black man wore a red bow tie.

"That looks stupid," said Nia uncomfortably, as if she sensed that, other than the color of his skin, the man on TV had nothing in common with us. One of the white men asked him how he thought something like the shooting could happen.

"Hear that?" Nia said. "He's making it sound like it's something that could never happen in his white world."

"The projects are a forgotten place that most people don't even know exists," the black man said.

"Or don't *want* to know exists," added the black woman.

"It's a hopeless cycle of broken families, illegitimate children, failed education, poverty, and lawlessness."

The twins sat on the floor sucking their thumbs, staring at the images on the TV. They couldn't have understood, but the rest of us in that cramped, hot little room did. That was our world they were talking about. We were that broken family living on welfare and food stamps, with illegitimate children and school dropouts and gang members. We were the hopeless.

"They may look black, but they talk white," Gramma observed, as if that would somehow negate what had been said.

"Not one of them ever set foot in the projects, that's for sure," muttered Nia.

"Let's face it," said one of the white men on the TV. "It's survival of the fittest. Those who survive do so by their wits and pure animal instincts. It's the rule of the jungle. The asphalt jungle."

"Turn it off," Nia said.

LaRue got up and turned off the TV. The room went quiet. From outside came the distant sounds of traffic, rap music, and the screech of train wheels in the rail yard.

Animals . . .

A forgotten place . . .

Hopeless . . .

"Turn it back to *Cosby*," Gramma said. Soon the laugh track filled the room.

But no one in the room laughed.

LARUE

By day, politicians and other important people made speeches in front of television cameras about how they were going to rehabilitate the Frederick Douglass Project. But as soon as the sun went down and the reporters went home for dinner, it was the same old thing. Gunfire, fear, isolation.

"You believe that crap?" Terrell said on yet another night while we watched some white windbag in a suit talk about what he was going to do for our underprivileged, uneducated, uncivilized neighbors and friends. "They ain't gonna do nothing."

Nia came into the room with Xavier on her hip, her cell phone against her ear, and a frown on her face. "I've been waiting all day for him to call back. If I leave a message, he always calls back. Always."

"Maybe his phone's broke," said Gramma, bouncing Jayda on her knee.

Nia gave me and Terrell a worried look. "Any idea where he could be?" she asked.

"I could check a few spots," Terrell said.

"Why don't you do that?" Nia said. "And if you find him, tell him to call home right away."

Terrell had to go upstairs first. In the stairwell on the fourteenth floor, a Disciple sat with a sawed-off rifle across his knees. His chin was propped in his hand, and he was writing in a battered spiral notebook. It was Darius, from Terrell's baby gang, Soon To Shoot. Now he, too, was a Disciple.

When he saw me, he straightened up and gripped the rifle. "No one but Disciples past this point."

"Marcus knows him," Terrell said.

Darius shook his head. "No exceptions. Orders is orders."

"It's okay," I said to Terrell. "You go."

Terrell continued up the stairs. Darius relaxed and laid the rifle across his knees again.

"How long you been a Disciple?" I asked.

"A few weeks."

"Didn't used to have guards up here," I said.

Darius raised and dropped his shoulder and went back to scratching words into his notebook. Another wannabe rapper.

Terrell came back. "Marcus says it's okay."

Darius frowned uncertainly. "You sure?"

"Do I have to go back and get him?" Terrell asked. It was a subtle threat. Marcus would be none too pleased to be bothered about something so trivial.

Darius waved me past. There must have been half a dozen Disciples milling around on the fifteenth floor, including Bublz and Jules, who'd been jumped in the year before. Tension was thick, and gang members were speaking in hushed, hurried voices. More than one narrowed his eyes suspiciously when I passed with Terrell.

We went into Marcus's apartment and followed voices into the kitchen. Marcus, Jamar, and Tyrone were standing around the kitchen table, which was covered with guns and boxes of ammunition.

"When'd you last see LaRue?" Marcus asked me.

"This morning," I said.

"Was he strapped?"

"Didn't notice," I said. "He usually is."

"We gotta squad up and spill some blood," Jamar said to Marcus. "They want a war, they'll get a war."

"We need to know for certain first," Marcus said grimly. "He ain't even late yet."

"Come on, man," Jamar said. "LaRue ain't here. He ain't answered his phone all day. Where do you think he's at?"

"Somewhere else," Marcus barked, clearly displeased that Jamar was doubting him. "Maybe he stopped to see a girlfriend. Maybe he got pinched. Maybe he got ambushed by a crew that ain't Gentry. You want to start a war with the wrong enemy?"

"Gentry's the enemy no matter what," Jamar grumbled.

Marcus opened a flip phone and dialed. The room grew quiet. He let the phone ring five times, then snapped it shut.

"You each take a man and go look for him," he told Jamar and Tyrone. "Soon as you know anything, call me."

Jamar and Tyrone headed out.

"You want me to look too?" Terrell asked eagerly.

"I want you to sit on that bench like you're supposed to," Marcus snapped, annoyed.

"But—"

Marcus glared at him, and Terrell didn't finish the sentence. We headed back downstairs. At the third floor, I turned toward Gramma's, but Terrell grabbed my arm. "Come on. We're gonna find LaRue."

"But Marcus said—"

"Marcus wants me to grow old and die on that bench," Terrell hissed. "I'm gonna show him I'm better than that." He patted me on the shoulder. "We got each other's backs, DeShawn. Long as we stick together, we'll be okay."

I knew disobeying Marcus was a mistake, but Terrell was right about one thing—for Nia and Xavier and Jayda's sake, I wanted to find LaRue. And I wanted to find him alive.

Outside, the night air was chilly. Winter wasn't quite ready to give up and let spring in. Terrell started walking west, toward the Flats.

"Why this way?" I asked.

"The hobby center," Terrell said. "Sometimes he plays that Warhammer game and don't want anyone to know, so he turns his phone off."

Suddenly I remembered that when LaRue left the apartment that morning, he had that black plastic case with him. Relief filtered through me. I'd been scared that my sister had lost her man, and, like so many of us, those babies would never know their father.

We got to the hobby center. Inside, racks of comic books and shelves of action figures lined the walls. Terrell led me to the back where groups of teenagers were huddled over tables covered with Warhammer armies. Everything stopped when Terrell entered. They recognized his colors.

"Anyone seen LaRue?" Terrell asked.

"Who?" someone said.

"Medium size, long braids, diamond stud in his right ear," I said.

"He was here," a guy said. "Probably left ten minutes ago."

Terrell and I shared a puzzled look. If LaRue left, why hadn't we run into him on the street?

"Was he with anyone?" I asked.

The guys exchanged glances and shook their heads. Terrell jerked his thumb toward the door, and we left.

Pop! At the sound of the gunshot, we both ducked. Car doors slammed, and a low gray sedan shot out of an alley next to the hobby center and sped away. Terrell and I ran into the alley. In the shadows a body lay on the ground. My heart started racing, and I slowed down as if part of me didn't want to know. But I knew.

LaRue's hands were tied behind him, and he lay

curled up as if he'd been kneeling when they shot him. A single bullet through the back of his head. I felt something under my foot. Black-and-white beads were scattered on the ground. They'd broken the string on purpose. It was the Gentry Gangstas' way of letting us know who had pulled the trigger.

Terrell cursed, and I heard beeps as he dialed a number. Part of LaRue's forehead was gone. Even in death his eyes were squeezed shut. My head started throbbing.

"He knew what was coming," I muttered.

"Huh?" Terrell didn't understand.

"Look at his eyes. He knew they were gonna kill him. They made him kneel."

In the dim light, something glistened on LaRue's cheek. I reached down and touched the moisture. Tears. He'd been crying when they shot him. The throbbing in my head grew into pounding. I saw Xavier's and Jayda's expectant faces. And Nia's fretful eyes . . .

A car pulled into the alley. "Crap!" Terrell grunted. Thinking it might be Gentry, he pulled his gun and shielded his eyes. Car doors opened. The headlights stayed on. I couldn't see anything except the glare.

There were footsteps. Terrell backed away, and I felt a shadow as Marcus stood over me and LaRue. The pain made my head feel like it was going to explode. I felt my hands clench and everything went black. *"You killed him!"* I launched myself at Marcus.

The scuffle was short. In no time Marcus had me

tied up in his strong arms and hands. But I was still fighting, squirming and cursing. "You made him a runner! You got him killed!"

Marcus increased his grip, pinning my arms to my sides. I heard him say, "Put those guns away."

I opened my eyes. Jules and two other gangbangers had their guns out, ready to kill me if I did anything to Marcus. They hesitated, then did as they were told. I tried to twist out of Marcus's grip, but his hands were like steel clamps.

"What do you want us to do?" Jules asked.

Marcus nodded at LaRue's body. "Search his pockets."

"Don't touch him!" I started to struggle anew. *"Leave him alone!"*

Marcus clamped a hand over my mouth. I twisted and tried to get free, but he put an arm around my chest and squeezed until it was hard to breathe, forcing me to stop fighting. Jules went through LaRue's pockets and came up with a couple of crumpled dollar bills and a cell phone.

"Give it here." Still holding me with one arm, Marcus took the phone. For a split second his gaze settled on Terrell, and a frown formed on his face. "All of you, bounce. Now!"

Jules nodded at me. "What about him?"

"He's goin' with me," Marcus said.

"The hell I am!" Once again I tried to fight, but Marcus pushed me down face-first on the cold, wet pavement and twisted my arm behind my back. "That's

enough," he grunted, and held me until the others had gone. I felt his warm breath close to my ear. "I'm gonna let you go, and you ain't gonna do nothin' stupid, understand?"

When I didn't answer, he twisted my arm harder, and I felt the pain shoot up through my shoulder, like it was going to pop out of its joint. "You *feel* me?" he growled. Only this time it sounded more like a threat.

Trembling and seized with pain, I nodded. "Yes."

Marcus let go. "Get in the car."

I pushed myself up from the ground and looked at LaRue's body. "You're just gonna leave him like that?"

Marcus gritted his teeth. "I said, get in the car."

I did as I was told. Marcus looked over the backseat as he backed the Mercedes out of the alley. He drove about half a block and pulled over. I watched silently while he dialed 911 on LaRue's phone.

"There's a body in the alley of the nine hundred block of Whitmore," he told the operator, and gave her LaRue's name and address. Then he hung up, got out of the car, and dropped LaRue's phone to the ground. He crushed it with his foot and kicked the pieces into a storm drain.

Back in the car, he said, "Get this straight. LaRue was a runner because he *wanted* to be a runner. There's only three ways up—treasurer, enforcer, or runner. We're okay in the treasurer department, and LaRue didn't want to be no enforcer, and that's that."

I sat in the front seat, silent, arms crossed. People

in this country were supposed to have choices. Wasn't that what America was about? Freedom to choose? But when you grew up in the projects, there were no choices. No good ones, at least.

I thought Marcus would start the car, but he didn't. "You think LaRue liked living in that apartment with you and your gramma? A man wants a crib of his own. He wants a ride and enough bank to keep his babies in Pampers and go out at night if he chooses."

"What happens to my sister and her babies now?" I asked.

Marcus drummed his fingers against the steering wheel, then reached into his pocket and pulled out a wad of cash. He thumbed off a bunch of bills and handed them to me.

The distant wail of a siren broke the silence. A cop car with flashing lights came up the block and turned down the alley. Marcus started the car and we drove away.

"How come you waited?" I asked.

"To make sure the right people found the body."

HYPE

No stories about the execution-style murder of a seventeen-year-old gangbanger and father of two appeared on TV or in the newspapers. No politicians made speeches. But two weeks later when a blond eighteen-year-old college freshman disappeared in Mexico while on spring break, it was all over the TV for days until she was found dazed and dirty, but otherwise okay, on a street corner.

Gramma's funeral insurance paid for the burial. She didn't have life or health or any other kind of insurance, but every month she paid forty-eight dollars to cover the cost of a funeral in case one of us died. When Nia became pregnant, she'd added LaRue to the policy. In her mind the worst and most undignified thing that could happen was to end up in the potter's field, the place where the city put the lost souls who had no families or money for a "proper" burial.

Nia stayed in bed and cried for days while Gramma and I took care of the twins. After a week she went down to social services and applied for support, but they said it would be months before the paperwork

went through. So each day, she left the babies with
Gramma and went upstairs where Marcus gave her a
job processing crack.

Then Gramma came down with shingles. We had
to prop her up with pillows on the couch. The disease
gave her blisters on her face and arms, but the worst
part was the pain. She'd wince and moan, and we knew
it was bad because usually she never complained about
anything. It was so bad that she didn't even care about
watching *Judge Joe Brown*.

I called the clinic, and they said they had medicine
that would help. The next morning the sun was out,
and the air felt warm and moist. There were even some
robins hopping around the yard, trying to pull worms
out of the dirt. I was walking along Abernathy when I
ran into Lightbulb with his head bowed and a sad look
in his eyes. He didn't notice me until I was just a few
yards away.

"What's wrong?" I asked.

He looked up, surprised, then hung his head.
"Snoop's gone."

"Sorry, man."

"Wanna help me look for him?"

"Can't. I got to go down to the clinic and get medicine for my gramma."

Lightbulb nodded. "Catch you later."

"Hope you find him."

I got Gramma's medicine and was leaving the clinic
when I noticed a beat-up, old, white Cadillac Seville

across the street. A skinny hype girl got out. It was morning, and she was wearing a short skirt and red high heels and lots of makeup, so it was obvious what she did to support her habit. I started to look away and then did a double take. It was Laqueta.

She crossed the street, her ankles wobbly in those red high heels, and went through the special clinic door where junkies got their methadone. Meanwhile the Seville stayed parked with its motor running. It was a sorry-looking vehicle. The red fabric on the roof was torn, one fender was crushed, a headlight was missing, and an old, sun-bleached "for sale" sign hung in the rear window.

Laqueta came out of the clinic and went back to the car, but she didn't get in. She leaned in the window and handed the driver a small bottle of red liquid. In return he slid her some dead presidents.

The car pulled away. Laqueta looked across the street and our eyes met. Her eyebrows dropped as she recognized me and probably realized I'd seen what she'd just done. Then her face changed. She raised one eyebrow and licked her red lips. I turned away and headed home.

Back at the apartment, I gave Gramma the medicine and then headed out to the yard. Terrell was in his usual spot on the bench.

"S'up?" he said.

"Just saw Laqueta down at the clinic selling her methadone. She's a hype now?"

Terrell bristled. "She had a hard time. Her little boy fell out that window, and Jamar dumped her."

"So that makes it okay?"

"No, it don't make it okay," said Terrell. "I'm just saying, that's all."

"Know what else she's doing?"

Terrell narrowed his eyes. "What is this?"

"I'm just asking if you know what your cousin's doing for drug money," I said.

Terrell's jaw hardened. "Yeah. So what's your point?"

I stared at him. "Don't you get it? What're you doing on this bench?"

"You know what I'm doing."

"You think Laqueta'd be a junkie-hooker if it wasn't for gangbangers like you out here selling dope?"

"What she does is her business," Terrell muttered with a shrug.

But I was still in his face. "No, man, it's *your* business. You're the one making money while she's out selling herself. And for what? So you can get a little bling? Go to a club on Saturday night and find some new skank to get pregnant?"

Terrell and I glared at each other. We were lifelong friends. The only real friend each other had. But lately I'd begun to wonder. "This is cold-blooded, Terrell. You're making money off your own people. Off your own family, for God's sake."

"Maybe I ain't as high and mighty as you, okay?" Terrell shot back. "Laqueta's grown-up enough to make her own decisions. Meanwhile I'm trying to work my way up. Because it's either this or mopping floors at King Chicken with my peeps coming in and laughing at me. And I don't know what you think you're doing that's any better."

"What I'm *not* doing is selling the same drugs my cousin's addicted to."

"And what *are* you doing instead, schoolboy?" Terrell sneered. "Gonna stay in Munson until you graduate? And then what? Get yourself a job working in some factory? Or driving a truck? With guys like Marcus making more in a day than you make in a month? Wait a minute, schoolboy. How come you ain't in school today?"

"Had to go to the clinic and get my gramma some medicine."

"So? The day ain't over. You can still go."

He was right. And the truth was, I wasn't at school because I didn't feel like going. It was the first nice day of spring, and I wanted to be outside. Besides, school wasn't leading anywhere. Most of the time I only went to see Tanisha. More and more I couldn't connect the things they were teaching us with life as I knew it. What difference did it make that Earth was on tectonic plates that sometimes moved and caused earthquakes and tsunamis? There were no earthquakes around here. Who cared what dead crackers like Mark Twain and Shakespeare wrote? How did any of that matter when all I saw around me was unemployment, drugs, and death?

Terrell raised his hand in an offer of truce, and I felt the anger start to drain away. Maybe he was right. Who was I to criticize him? All of us were stuck here, just trying to survive. He took out a pinner, lit it, and offered me some. Despite everything I'd just said, I took a hit. Sometimes it was the only way to cope.

"Face it, DeShawn," Terrell wheezed as he exhaled sweet smoke. "This is all there is."

MONEY

"It's been a long time since we went out," Tanisha whispered in my ear. We were lying on a mattress on the floor of an abandoned building near Munson High. Kids used the place to skip school, get high, and hook up. The mattress was filthy and stank, but Tanisha kept clean sheets hidden in a garbage bag in a hole in the wall.

"We go out and get seen, I get killed," I whispered back, stroking her cheek.

"Only around here," she said. "We could meet downtown. Or on the South Side where nobody knows us."

I couldn't blame her. For months the only places she and I had been together were school and this drafty old building with boarded-up windows and broken glass and garbage all over the floors. But being seen wasn't the only problem with going out.

"Gramma's sick, and Nia's welfare checks ain't started yet," I said. "We're already behind on the rent and cable."

"I've got money," Tanisha said. "All those nights I can't see you, I babysit."

I felt my heart twist. Most girls wouldn't put up

with a guy who couldn't show them a good time on Saturday night. Tanisha was different, and what we shared was special. Special enough for me to risk my life to see her.

"What's for dinner?" Gramma asked from the couch. Even with the medicine, she could hardly move without pain, so it was up to Nia and me to cook.

"Let me check," I said, even though I knew there was hardly anything. The money Marcus had given us was gone. The night before, we'd had rice and ketchup, and at least once a day Nia had to give the twins sugar water instead of formula.

I went into the kitchen. Nia was standing beside the counter, her head titled back and eyes closed, gulping something from a can in her hand. She finished with a sigh of satisfaction, then opened her eyes, saw me, and quickly hid the can behind her back.

Her face flushed and she turned her head, unable to face me. What could she be hiding? Had she become a wino without me noticing? Realizing there was no sense in pretending, she brought her hand out from behind her back and placed the can on the counter. It was baby formula.

"Don't tell Gramma," she whispered, her eyes brimming with tears of shame. "I was so hungry."

Now I saw what I'd missed before. My sister was skinnier than I'd ever seen her. Her cheeks were hollow, and her hands and wrists were bony. Anger rose up from deep inside, and I turned to leave.

As I went through the living room, Gramma said, "Where're you going?"

"To get some food."

Nia followed me through the front door and out into the hall. "You got money?" she whispered.

"No," I said. There was the money in the envelope Marcus had entrusted to me, but I'd given him my word. Facing that choice, I'd rather break the law.

"Then how?"

I turned away and headed downstairs, footsteps slapping, seething with fury, feeling like I wanted to hit someone or something as hard as I could. And that's what I figured I'd have to do, with a rock or a brick. Go down Abernathy a few blocks and wait by the intersection for the right car—one driven by some older white woman with a pocketbook on the seat beside her. Pretend I was crossing with the light and strike fast. Smash the window, grab the bag, and run. Just thinking about it made my heart thump hard and my head feel hot. It was a step down to a place I'd tried all my life not to go. But Gramma was sick, the babies needed food, and we were all hungry.

Was it fate that I ran into Terrell coming up the stairs? He was wearing a light blue and white University of North Carolina cap backward with a do-rag under it; a matching, oversize, blue and white UNC jersey; basketball shoes; and long denim shorts. He was listening to an iPod, and on his wrist was a gold-plated watch with a thick gold band. Plus he was carrying a shopping bag. I'd never seen him so tricked out.

"What'd you get?" I asked.

Terrell took a Nike box out of the bag and opened it. Inside were bright white basketball shoes. "Nice, huh?"

The blue and white basketball shoes on his feet were hardly scuffed. Meanwhile I had one pair of sneakers, and I had to keep them fresh with white shoe polish.

"S'up?" he asked.

"Got twenty I can borrow?"

Terrell smirked. "End of the month?"

The anger, which had momentarily vanished, came back fast and hard. I felt the urge to say something ugly but caught myself. "Forget it." I started down the stairs again.

"Whoa," Terrell called behind me. "How about King Chicken? On me."

I looked back up at him in his new clothes. "Thanks, but there's Nia and Gramma, too."

"Got it covered," Terrell said. "Come on up while I drop this off."

I didn't move. I didn't want his charity.

"Come on, DeShawn. How many times have you saved my sorry butt?"

Next thing I knew, I was climbing the stairs with him.

"Marcus is thinking about making me the new runner," he said.

"After what happened to LaRue?" I asked in disbelief. "You whack?"

"It's good money," Terrell said. "Big step up."

"You'll get yourself killed."

"That's the chance you take," Terrell said as if it meant nothing.

We got up to his apartment. Mrs. Blake wasn't there, but Laqueta and two guys were. The TV was on, and the table and floor were covered with bottles and ashtrays full of cigarette butts. Laqueta and her friends wore stained, ragged clothes and looked glassy-eyed.

"Gimme some money," Laqueta said languidly, as if she knew he wouldn't.

Terrell ignored her and went down the hall. His room had a new metal door secured with two padlocks. It was already dented and scratched, as if someone had tried to break through. I didn't have to ask who.

Terrell undid the locks. Inside was a flat-screen TV and a new sound system. New clothes with tags still on them were scattered around.

"I thought sitting on the bench didn't pay," I said, taking in all the swag.

"Not till I figured out the system," Terrell answered slyly. "I skim a little off every bag of weed and every vial of rock. Five bags becomes six. Same with the vials. End of the day, the money from the extras is all mine."

"Marcus know?" I asked.

"Probably. Only no one talks about it."

An open bag of peanuts lay on the desk. Terrell saw

me eyeing it. "Take as much as you want. The cousins is always sending us more."

I took a handful, and we left the apartment and walked to King Chicken. It was dinnertime, and the place was filled. We got in line. The scent of fried chicken made my stomach grumble.

I was studying the menu when a commotion started in a booth where a heavy lady sat with three shorties. One of the shorties had tipped over a supersize soda, spilling it all over the table and floor.

"Raydale!" the white-shirted manager called back into the kitchen. "Get the mop!"

When Lightbulb came out of the back wearing black pants and a stained, white shirt with the tails hanging out, Terrell and I were taken by surprise. He pushed a yellow bucket with a wooden broom handle sticking out of it. Seeing us, he stopped and grinned. "Hey!"

"How long you been working here?" Terrell asked.

"'Bout a month," Lightbulb said.

"What about school?" I asked.

Before Lightbulb could answer, the manager yelled, "Raydale! Did I say you could talk to your friends?"

Lightbulb hurried toward the booth and started mopping. Meanwhile the heavy woman pointed at the seats and started giving orders. "What about that there?" she asked irately, as if the spilled soda had been Lightbulb's fault.

"I'll get it." Lightbulb hurried into the kitchen and returned with a rag to wipe the seats.

"And that?" The woman pointed at the plates, cups, and buckets sitting in a sea of soda on the table.

Lightbulb started wiping the soda off the table, but as he did, it began spilling onto the floor and seats again.

"Watch what you doing, fool!" the woman yelled.

Her yelling flustered him. By now almost everyone in King Chicken had paused to watch. In a panic, Lightbulb swiped the towel across the table, splashing soda onto the woman's son's pants and shoes.

"Now look what you done!" the woman shrieked.

The commotion brought the manager out from behind the counter. "What's the problem, ma'am?"

"This fool's making a mess all over again," the woman complained. "He got soda all over my son." She pointed at her son's pants, which were practically soaked with soda from spilling the supersize cup in the first place.

"You did that?" the bewildered manager asked Lightbulb.

"No, sir," Lightbulb stammered.

"You calling me a liar?" the woman bellowed.

"No, ma'am, I'm sure he's just mistaken," the manager quickly said. "I'll be glad to replace any food that was spoiled. Why don't you take a seat over here?" He showed her to an empty table, then said to Lightbulb, "As soon as you finish cleaning up this mess, I want to see you in the back."

Lightbulb hung his head like a scolded puppy. He finished wiping and mopping and went into the back. I hated the way they treated him. I hated seeing someone so smart working such a lousy job. But I was hungry and it was our turn to order. I got a big bucket of chicken with some sides of mashed potatoes. Terrell got a meal to go and paid for everything. We headed back toward Douglass.

"Guess you could always get a job at King Chicken," Terrell said with a chuckle.

NO CHOICE

Back home I was a big hero. Gramma, Nia, and I sat around the TV and dug in hungrily while the twins played on the floor. The funny thing was, the three of us together couldn't finish that one bucket of chicken. I guess that's how much our stomachs had shrunk from hunger.

After dinner I headed upstairs. As I climbed, I thought about Lightbulb being yelled at in King Chicken. I thought about Tanisha and the smelly mattress we had to share in that drafty, cold building. I thought about school, where kids spent all day clowning and socializing, most of them there only because there was no place else to go. I thought about all the pregnant girls having babies. I thought about all the gangbangers living for the minute because they might be dead in an hour.

The people who sat around tables on TV, wearing suits and talking cracker English, might say there was a choice.

The teachers who came for a year and then disappeared forever might want to think there was a choice.

The politicians looking for excuses to get on TV

might want people to believe they were going to give folks like us a choice.

But everyone knew the truth: There was no choice.

Not when the only world you knew was the projects.

Upstairs Jules was sitting on the steps, the sawed-off rifle across his lap, with his chin on his hand, looking bored. "What do you want?"

"Marcus here?" I asked.

"He's busy."

"Tell him it's DeShawn."

One of Jules's eyebrows went up and the other went down. "So?"

"You don't tell him, I will." I started to go around him. Jules sprang to his feet and aimed the rifle at me. I stopped, but I didn't feel scared. I was sick of people aiming guns at me. I was sick of not having money and being hungry at the end of each month. I was sick of being alone in the world and being the man of the house with an ailing gramma and a widowed sister with two babies, and having a girlfriend I could only see on the down low.

"You gonna shoot me?" I asked, and realized part of me almost wished he would put me out of my misery.

"I *told* you he's busy," Jules said.

"And I'm telling *you* I don't care," I said, and continued past him.

"Don't," Jules said, keeping the gun trained on me.

"I saved your sorry butt twice," I said, and kept going. "You ain't shooting me."

Jules followed. "Marcus is gonna kill you for bothering him. And he's gonna kill me for letting you."

Music was coming from inside Marcus's apartment. I rapped my knuckles hard against the door. Jules hung back as if to stay clear of whatever mayhem was about to come.

There was no answer. I knocked again and glanced at Jules. It seemed like his grip on the rifle had gotten tighter.

"Don't get nervous and accidentally pull that trigger," I said.

"You don't know what you doing," he hissed.

I knocked again. This time harder and longer. I heard a door bang inside and then the thud of footsteps across a floor. "Who's there?" Marcus's voice was loud and annoyed.

"DeShawn."

There was a moment of silence, then bolts on the other side of the door clinked. Out of the corner of my eye, I saw Jules take another step back.

The door swung open, and Marcus stood there bare chested with bare feet and his big black gun in his hand. It looked like he'd taken just enough time to pull on a pair of pants but not enough time to buckle the belt. Behind him a woman wrapped in a white sheet stood in the bedroom doorway. Marcus scowled at me, then turned and glowered at Jules.

"I tried to stop him," Jules stammered. "I swear."

"He did," I said. "But I told him he'd have to shoot me."

Marcus's thick eyebrows dipped. He told Jules to go back to his post. I took a white envelope out of my jacket. With a frown, Marcus slid the gun into his waistband.

He blinked, almost as if he'd forgotten about it. "Never told a soul, did you?"

"No, sir." I held it out for him to take. "You said it couldn't be kept by a Disciple."

Marcus stared at me for a moment.

"You sure?"

"Uh-huh."

"All right, but you can keep that."

"But—"

A crooked, knowing smile broke through his lips. "Open it."

I did as I was told. Except for the fifty and the one-hundred dollar bill he'd shown me the day he had given it to me, the rest of the bills were all ones. It took me a moment to understand—it had been a test.

"Stay here." Marcus went back into the apartment, then returned. "Turn around."

A string of black-and-white beads went around my neck, and Marcus tied them in the back. It reminded me of the day he'd tied my tie. "Come back in an hour and we'll talk."

Downstairs in our apartment, Gramma and Nia were watching TV. My sister had the twins beside her, both sucking hungrily at bottles of sugar water. I gestured for her to join me in the kitchen and gave her the hundred-dollar bill from the envelope.

Nia's eyes widened. "Where'd you get this?"

I pulled down the neck of my T-shirt and showed her the beads.

SIXTEEN YEARS OLD

Young, unemployed black men murder one another at nine times the rate of white youths. In 1965, 24 percent of black infants were born to single mothers. By 1990 the rate had risen to 64 percent. In 2005 it was just under 70 percent.

"STILL I'M SAYIN' WHY DO WE RESIDE
IN THE GHETTO WITH A MILLION WAYS TO DIE?"
—FROM "EVERY GHETTO" BY NAS

SHOOT OUT

Tanisha and I continued to see each other. William moved in with a girlfriend, and Tanisha hardly saw him anymore. At my place the twins were crawling now, and the apartment felt even smaller and more cramped. None of the promises the politicians made on TV came true. I heard somewhere that the ten- and nine-year-old shooters had been charged with murder and were being held in juvie.

Laqueta died from an overdose. Darius, the Disciple and wannabe rapper, was arrested for armed robbery. Precious and Imani both had babies, but now Terrell was hanging around a girl named Ambrosia.

"Who needs ammo?" Jamar asked at a meeting on the fifteenth floor. Since gangbangers were shooting almost every day, they always needed more. Even though we were all in the same gang, we still had to pay.

"A dollar a bullet?" Jules sputtered. "How come we got to pay so much?"

"You got to pay that much because I got to pay that much," Jamar said.

"That why you're driving a new Escalade?" Tyrone asked.

"You don't like it, get your ammo somewhere else," Jamar said.

"Whose side you on, anyway?" asked Jules.

Jamar began to move his lip, but then stopped and stared at the doorway. Marcus had entered the room. He looked at everyone and his eyes settled on Jamar. "A dollar's too high," he said.

"But—" Jamar started to protest, then caught himself and gave Marcus a hard look.

Marcus ignored him. "You heard me."

Marcus had me sit in on meetings with Jamar and other high-level gang members, while street-level souljas and dealers older than me were kept out. My job was to be quiet and listen.

"How much?" Marcus asked one night in his apartment when Jamar brought in a gun dealer who had three AK-47s to sell. The dealer, Jamar, and Marcus were sitting in the deep, black leather chairs in front of his flat-screen TV. A basketball game was on, the sound muted. I sat in a corner, playing Underground Racer on my cell phone.

"Twelve hundred each," said the dealer. "But I can hook you up with all three for three g's flat."

"It's a good deal," Jamar said. "These guns got a Hellfire switch to turn 'em automatic. You can empty a fifty clip in five seconds. Nobody gonna mess with that kind of firepower. Nobody."

"I'll think about it," Marcus said.

From my seat in the corner, I glanced up, curious to see how Jamar would take that reply. I expected that he'd be looking at Marcus or the dealer or the TV screen. But he wasn't. He was staring at me with a frown on his face. I looked back down at my cell phone.

Jamar told the dealer to go out into the hall and wait. He closed the door and returned to the couch and Marcus. "We don't buy those guns, you know who will," he whispered urgently. "The Gentry boys get a hold of those things, they'll walk right over us."

Marcus nodded gravely.

"So?" Jamar asked impatiently.

"Go out in the hall and give me a minute," Marcus said.

"What?" Jamar sounded surprised. I couldn't remember Marcus ever sending him out before.

"You heard me."

I kept my gaze on my cell phone, but I had a feeling that if I'd looked up, it would have been into Jamar's eyes.

Marcus waited until Jamar left, then picked up the clicker and turned up the sound. The roar of the basketball crowd filled the room while he went into the kitchen. Returning with two beers, he gestured for me to join him. "What do you think?" he asked in a low voice. Anyone out in the hall trying to listen would have heard only the game.

I twisted the top off my beer and took a gulp. "I'm

thinking maybe that dealer has more than three AKs. Maybe he has six."

Marcus tapped his knuckles against his chin. "If we don't buy three, what stops him from selling all six to the Gangstas?"

"He sells six to the Gangstas, those'll be the last guns he'll sell around here for a long time," I said.

Marcus kept tapping. "So you think the only way he can keep selling guns is if he keeps the sides even? And I think maybe you're right, but what if you're wrong?"

I had an idea and leaned close, whispering.

A few moments later, when Marcus invited Jamar and the dealer back into the apartment, I was once again sitting in the corner, playing with my cell phone. Marcus and the others sat down in the chairs near the TV.

"I want six," Marcus said.

Jamar and the gun dealer exchanged startled glances.

"He's only got three," Jamar said.

Marcus ignored him and spoke to the dealer. "And I'm willing to pay fifteen hundred each."

Seeing big dollar signs, the dealer took the bait. "I might be able to get three more."

"You *sure?*" Jamar challenged him with obvious disapproval.

The dealer hesitated, as if sensing he'd made a mistake. "Well, uh . . ."

"Nine g's for the six," Marcus said.

The dealer's eyes darted at Jamar, who stared back coldly at him. But the lure of an easy nine thousand dollars was too much. "Half now, half on delivery?"

Marcus got up and went into the bedroom. I kept my eyes on my cell phone. A few moments later he came back, and I heard the slither of dead presidents being counted.

Thanks to the Disciples, I had money now. Enough to pay the rent and make sure the twins had Pampers and baby food. Gramma had gotten over the shingles, but instead of going back to cleaning houses, she took care of the twins. Nia went to school once in a while, but she spent most of her time with Tyrone, her new boyfriend. When he wasn't gangbanging, Tyrone was scratching out lyrics—yet another wannabe rap star.

Tanisha and I saw each other at the abandoned building, and now and then in school, although I hardly showed up anymore. On Saturday nights we would take separate buses and meet downtown to have dinner and go to clubs.

"What's wrong?" I asked at dinner one night when she was being quiet. We were sitting in a dark red leather booth at the back of an Italian restaurant. A candle flickered on the table between us. I was wearing a new, pin-striped, gray suit and a black shirt. Tanisha was wearing a black dress.

She glanced down at her plate. Her veal Parmesan was untouched. In the candlelight, her skin glowed warmly and her hair had a sheen. To me, she was the most beautiful girl in the world.

"Come on, Tani, tell me."

Her eyes met mine. "William knows something's going on. All of a sudden he's coming around. And calling at strange times. If I get home late from school, he wants to know where I've been. If I say I'm going babysitting, he wants to know for who. I'm scared, DeShawn."

"Of what?" I reached across the table and took her hand.

"You know."

"That he'll come after me?"

"That he'll *kill* you," Tanisha said in a low voice. "You heard him say so yourself."

"That's what he has to say."

Tanisha leaned forward and cupped my hand with both hers. Her face took on an urgent expression. "It's what he'd have to *do*, DeShawn. The Gangstas would insist on it."

That was true. It was unacceptable to have a sister dating the enemy. Especially when you were as high up in the organization as William. It was the only way he could prove his loyalty. But I didn't want Tanisha to worry. "I can take care of myself."

Her eyes grew glittery. "If anything happened to you . . ."

I squeezed her hands in mine. "Nothing's gonna happen."

"You don't know."

"I never take the same route two days in a row," I said. "I hardly ever leave Frederick Douglass except to see you."

Tanisha pressed her lips together hard. "Couldn't we go away?"

That caught me by surprise. "You mean, take a trip?"

"No, I mean, for good. Some place where there are no gangs."

"Where?" I asked.

"I don't know. Don't you have any relatives anywhere?"

All the relatives I had were right in Frederick Douglass. The only life I'd ever known was Frederick Douglass. I couldn't imagine leaving Gramma and Nia and my friends and going off to some strange place.

"We'll be okay," I said, trying to reassure her. "I promise."

Tanisha bowed her head. We didn't say anything more about it. But she hardly touched her food.

After dinner we went to the Cheeta Club. We'd been there a few times before, and it was a good place to dance and have a few drinks. While the Italian restaurant wouldn't serve us wine with dinner because we were underage, we had no trouble getting served in the club.

The Cheeta was loud and dark except for the flashing lights that burst on and off. I led Tanisha to the bar.

"What do you feel like?" I asked.

"Ginger ale."

"That's all?" Usually she had a Seven and Seven or a rum and Coke. "Come on, loosen up. This is the only night of the week we get to have fun. Nothing bad's gonna happen."

But Tanisha insisted on ginger ale. Afterward we danced until it was time to go, then squeezed into a dark doorway near the bus stop and kissed. It was late and the streets were empty. The night air was warm, and a few of the brighter stars were visible in the dark sky. When the bus's headlights appeared several blocks away, our kisses grew more passionate.

The bus arrived. I began to let go, but Tanisha held on tightly.

"I love you," she whispered. It was the first time.

"I love you, too," I whispered back.

The driver looked at us impatiently. Tanisha eased her grip and backed away. "Be careful." She climbed on and took the closest seat to the bus driver. The doors closed. Tanisha waved through the window and blew me a kiss.

Having made sure Tanisha got on her bus first, I stood alone at the dark bus stop. Fortunately the bus would stop right in front of her building, so she wouldn't have a long walk in the dark when she got back to Gentry. A siren wailed in the distance and some car horns honked. Tanisha was right. We couldn't keep going this way. Sooner or later the wrong people were going to find out.

A dozen yards away, a car pulled up to the corner, its headlights illuminating a graffiti-covered store gate across the street. A cab passed, then an old man with a scruffy beard rode by on a rickety, old bike singing to himself.

It grew quiet again. The car at the corner hadn't moved. The engine was running and the lights were still on. As I watched out of the corner of my eye, a window came down, and I saw the silhouette of someone inside. My heart began banging and rattling. A faint glimmer of something metallic appeared.

I dived.

Pow! It was too loud to be a handgun or a rifle. Only a shotgun made a burst like that. If I had any doubts, the "Zing! Ping!" of ricocheting buckshot confirmed my suspicion.

Screech! Tires screamed as the car tore around the corner and came down the block toward me.

I jumped to my feet and thought for an instant about running, but the car would beat me wherever I went. Instead, I stood sideways behind a lamppost and pulled my gun, a ten-shot TEC .38.

Pow! Whizz! Clink! Ping! Clang! The second shotgun blast was a flash of light, and more buckshot zinged past my head. Pellets ricocheted off the lamppost. Blood pounding in my ears, I slipped the safety off the TEC, worked the slide back, and jacked the first round into the chamber. Then, hands locked together, I raised the gun, arms sweeping with the movement of the car, my heart banging almost as hard as the gunshots themselves. *Bang! Bang! Bang!* I fired three shots. A window shattered. The car skidded sideways, out of control, fishtailing left and right, then came to a stop in the middle of the street. I stayed behind the lamppost, trying to hold my gun steady despite my shaking hands and thudding heart.

Someone moved inside the car, but it was too dark to see. I heard muttering and curses. The windshield wipers went on and off, as if someone had pushed the wrong lever. Then the car started moving again. This time, away, down the street.

JUST A BOY

I spent the rest of the night curled on the floor under a staircase in some building. Couldn't risk going back out into the dark. The shooters in that car might have come back, or they might have called in their friends. I kept thinking about the way Tanisha had acted at dinner. How worried and scared she'd been. Almost like she knew something bad might happen.

If I slept, it wasn't for long. By the time the lobby began filling with natural light, footsteps were coming down the stairs—the heavy thumps of men going to work, the softer steps of women, and the taps of children. This wasn't the projects. It was a part of town where people had regular jobs and schedules. Where men and women came home at night, and kids went to school until high school was completed.

When there were a lot of people on the sidewalk outside, I crawled out from under the staircase. One of my pant's knees was torn, and my new suit was dirty and wrinkled. The tails of my shirt hung out, and the palms of my hands were scraped from diving to the ground the night before.

I tucked in my shirt and gazed down at the gun in my hand. I'd kept it close during the night just in case, but now I'd have to get rid of it. If I'd hit someone in that car, I didn't want the cops to be able to trace the bullet back to me. I was sliding the gun into my waistband holster when the door to one of the ground-floor apartments opened. A woman came out with two little kids dressed in clean clothes and carrying backpacks for school. The woman gasped when she saw the gun, then protectively reached for her kids and drew them back.

"It's cool," I said. "I'm going."

Holding the kids close, the woman frowned and her mouth began to move. I tensed, expecting her to say something angry, but she said, "You're . . . you're just a boy."

Her words caught me by surprise, and I didn't know how to answer. Maybe it was true. People said I looked young for my age, but it had been a long time since I'd felt like "just a boy."

"That no good Jamar," Marcus muttered that evening in his car. "I told him I wanted him for this."

I didn't ask where we were going. Marcus would tell me when he wanted me to know. The evening was damp and chilly. Wet spring mist hung in the air and covered everything, making streetlamps glitter and cars look dull. Marcus drove past the rail yards and into a part of town I'd never been in before. It was mostly old, brick factory buildings with broken windows and boarded-up doors.

He stopped the car beside an empty lot. I looked out at the rubble and mounds of garbage bags that had been discarded there. Poking out of the pile was a red pedal-car like the one I used to drive around the apartment when I was little.

Marcus took out his phone and tried a number. It rang until the message came on. He snapped the phone shut, then propped an elbow against the steering wheel, made a fist, and pressed it against his forehead. His eyes were closed, and I knew he was thinking hard, searching for a solution to whatever problem had beset him. For the first time ever, I sensed he was scared. Finally he took his fist from his forehead and opened his eyes.

"Got your gun?" he asked, staring out into the dark.

"No."

He turned and looked at me. "What? Why not?"

"I had to use it last night, and I threw it away."

"Use it how?"

"Someone took a shot at me."

Marcus frowned. "Who?"

"Don't know. It was dark. They were in a car."

"You shoot back? Think you hit anyone?"

"Might have," I said.

Marcus reached across to the glove compartment, pulled out a chrome-plated gun with a tan grip, and handed it to me. It was a .44 caliber. "Get in the back and stay down."

I did as I was told, and Marcus started to drive again. "We're gonna pick up those AK-47s. You stay in the car.

Anything goes wrong, you know what to do."

I crouched down in the space between the seats. The grip of the .44 slowly grew warm in my hand. The car turned and bounced slightly, as if going into a driveway. It stopped and Marcus got out. I stayed low and listened. There were voices. Someone asked Marcus if he'd come alone and he answered yes. Then someone else spoke. It sounded like Jamar. I raised my head and peeked around the headrest. It was dark, and we were in a parking lot behind some buildings. Marcus was talking to Jamar and the gun dealer. There was something strange about Jamar, and at first I couldn't tell what it was. Then I realized from the way his jacket was draped over his shoulders that his arm must have been in a sling. I couldn't hear what they were saying, but the conversation continued. It sounded low-key and chatty. Crouched behind the car seat, I relaxed and yawned.

Pop!

The sound of the shot made me jump. My first impulse was to stretch up and see what had happened. But something told me not to. If it was Jamar and Marcus and the gun dealer, then it had to be the dealer who got it, right? But I wasn't sure, so I stayed low and waited. Someone muttered. A shoe scraped against the asphalt. I slowly lifted my head and peeked. Jamar and the gun dealer were walking toward Jamar's black Escalade on the other side of the parking lot. I stretched up just a hair more and caught my breath.

Marcus lay on the asphalt.

"Anything goes wrong," he'd said, *"you know what to do."*

What did that mean? If Jamar had killed Marcus, I knew what to do. *But not now. Not here.* Not when it was two against one. And not before I knew why and what was going on. So I huddled in Marcus's car and waited until I heard the Escalade leave, then got out. Marcus lay facedown on the wet asphalt, a small hole in the back of his head and a spreading puddle of blood on the ground.

Light mist floated down in the dark. I could feel it seeping into my hair. At my feet lay the one person I never thought would die. The one who would always be there to tell us what to do. As I stood there I imagined the spark of life sputtering out like a flickering flame. Marcus was gone and he was never coming back. Could he really be just another gangbanger, as meaningless and simply forgotten as yesterday's weather? Was that the fate of all of us? Were we all nothing more than a brief flicker, as easily blown out as a candle?

The pool of blood under his head kept growing. I kneeled down and pressed my hand against his lifeless back. I felt tears well in my eyes. He'd been a gang leader and a killer, but he'd also been more like a father to me than any man I'd ever known. He was one of the few who'd given me a chance to be something. One of the few who hadn't left. I owed him. I would find out why Jamar had killed him. I would figure out what to do next.

DO WHAT'S RIGHT

Staying in the misty shadows, I took the dark side streets home. There was no telling who might see me if I walked down Abernathy Avenue. By the time I got back to Frederick Douglass, the mist had soaked my hair and seeped down under my collar, chilling me as it crept down my back. I was crossing the yard when my cell phone rang. It was Jamar.

"Come up."

"What's up?" I pretended not to know.

"Something happened to Marcus," he said.

I slid my hand inside my jacket and felt the grip of the .44. There was always a chance Jamar wanted me dead too. It could have been him who'd tried to kill me at the bus stop the night before.

I climbed up the stairs slowly, stopping and checking before going around each corner. By the time I got to the fifteenth floor, most of the Disciples were already there, talking in hushed voices and looking agitated. Terrell came over to me.

"They got Marcus," he whispered. "We're squadding up. They got to fall. Jamar got some AKs. We're gonna hurt them twice as bad."

"*Who* got Marcus?" I asked.

"Who do you think?"

All around the room, gangbangers were talking war. Then Jamar strutted in, his arm in a black sling. When our eyes met, he looked away.

"We going to war, right?" said Jules.

"Shut it and listen up," Jamar barked. "We ain't going to war. Least not right now. Marcus got shot by some crazy hype."

"You whack?" said Terrell. "Everybody knows Marcus. Ain't no hype anywhere would touch him."

"Look, I'm telling you it was some hype," Jamar insisted. "Marcus got soft. He lost respect. It ain't the same as it used to be."

"So what're we gonna do?" Bublz asked, nervously chewing a fingernail.

"Nothing," Jamar said.

A puzzled hush settled over the group.

"Only now you're in charge?" I asked.

Jamar locked eyes with me, then looked around the room. "Anyone got a problem with that?"

The other Disciples averted their eyes and shook their heads silently.

"All right," said Jamar. "Then it's back to business as usual. Nothing changes. Only I give the orders from now on."

Terrell and I started down the stairs. I waited until we were almost to the sixth floor and then stopped him.

"I gotta tell you something," I said in a low voice.

"You gotta swear not to tell anyone else, understand? This is on our blood oath. It's the most serious thing I'm ever gonna tell you, and if you tell a soul, it'll probably get me killed."

Terrell nodded and gave me a curious look.

"You were right before," I said. "Marcus wasn't killed by a hype. You and I know darn well that if some hype did it, the first thing Jamar would do was have him killed."

Terrell's eyebrows jumped as he realized this was true. "Then who? . . ."

"Jamar."

Terrell's jaw fell open and his forehead wrinkled. "But—"

I held up my hand to stop him. "I was there. It was an ambush. Jamar doesn't know I saw him."

My friend's face went stony. "You don't want to tell the others?"

"They won't believe me," I said. "Or some will and some won't, and then we'll have a war among ourselves."

"Folks know you don't lie."

I shook my head. "This is too big. They won't know what to believe. They might think I'm trying to take over. That after Jamar I'd be next in line. Besides, if anyone tells Jamar, he'll have me killed for sure."

Terrell's eyes wrinkled slightly. "Why you telling me?"

"If anything happens to me, I need you to know why, and to do what's right," I said.

A SECRET MEETING

The next morning, I got up early and went out unarmed for the first time in months. It was too soon for the funeral notices for Marcus to start going up in the stairwells. I walked to Munson High.

At the entrance, I was stopped by Mr. White, the fat, bald assistant principal whose stomach fell over his belt. "DeShawn, what an unexpected surprise," he said. "What brings you to school today?"

There was no point in lying. It was the first time I'd been to school in two weeks. "Just want to see my girl, Mr. White."

"At least you're honest," he said. "Go to my office and wait for me there."

I did as I was told. He showed up about twenty minutes later, sat down, and typed on the computer. "Let's see. Ah, here we are. In the past two months, you've missed twenty-seven days of school. Not exactly a stellar attendance record, is it?"

I didn't answer. I'd already told him why I was there.

Mr. White scratched the side of his face. "School's

not supposed to be a place where we come just to socialize, DeShawn. And you can't learn very much when your attendance averages one day a week."

I nodded.

"Do you have a job?" he asked.

"No, sir."

"May I ask what you do with your free time?"

We both knew exactly what I did.

Mr. White picked up a pencil and tapped it against his desk. "You're from Douglass?"

"Yes, sir."

"There's a boy in your grade from over there. Extraordinarily bright."

"Lightbulb."

"Sorry?"

"Raydale," I said. "Raydale Diggs."

"You know him?"

"He's working at King Chicken," I said. Lightbulb had worked his way up to the counter. He knew the price of every item by heart, and no matter how complicated the order, he automatically added it up in his head and calculated the tax and change. The manager constantly had to remind him to use the cash register anyway.

Mr. White shook his head sadly. "So much wasted potential. They talk about inner-city crime. But the real crime is what happens to boys like him and you." He glanced at the computer and back at me. "You're not here to make any trouble?"

"No, sir."

"You can talk to your girlfriend at lunch and in the hall between classes, but I don't want any reports of you hanging around where you're not supposed to be."

"Yes, sir."

"If you ever decide you really want to come back to school in a serious way, I can help you."

"Thank you, sir."

"Get your brother to arrange a meeting between me and Rance," I said. Tanisha and I were standing in a doorway outside the cafeteria. It was raining, but as long as we stood close to the doors, we wouldn't get wet.

"Are you crazy?" Tanisha said, hugging herself for warmth.

"Serious as I can be."

"He'll kill you."

"Maybe not."

"Maybe definitely."

"It's important, Tani."

"Not as important as you staying alive," she said.

"Tell him we can meet somewhere neutral."

"He won't do it."

"Tanisha, you gotta *make* him do it."

"I can't."

I moved close and put my hands on her hips, holding her steady and looking into her eyes. "Tani, you ever want the day to come when you and me can be together?"

Her eyes began to glitter. "We can't be together if you're dead."

"We can't be together while I'm alive, either," I said. "Unless you help me."

Walking home, I became aware of a car slowly moving along Abernathy. My hand automatically went to my waist, then I remembered that I wasn't strapped. I glanced out the corner of my eye. It was a dark green Crown Victoria, a favorite among undercover cops. In a way that was good news, and I relaxed. It was unlikely that a cop would take a shot at me.

The window went down. "Hey, DeShawn." It was Officer Patterson, wearing a green plaid jacket. "Congratulate me. I made detective."

I kept walking. He had to be crazy to think I'd speak to him. If anyone saw us, I was a dead man.

"Looks like we're both rising in our respective organizations," Patterson said.

At the corner, I stopped and waited for traffic to pass. But I didn't look at him.

"Meet me under the rail-yard bridge in twenty minutes," Patterson said. "We need to talk." The Crown Vic pulled away.

Twenty minutes later I walked toward the bridge. I'd taken a roundabout route through abandoned buildings and over backyard fences, so I was pretty sure I wasn't followed. The rail-yard bridge was low and made of stone. It was dark and damp and rat-infested underneath. Even homeless people wouldn't sleep there.

Patterson was standing in the shadows. No sign of the Crown Vic or anyone else. I walked in and stopped half a dozen yards away from him. Water dripped from the ceiling into puddles, and I thought I heard rats scampering in the dark corners.

"I won't keep you long," Patterson said. "I know what would happen if anyone in your crew found out."

I looked around uncomfortably.

"No one's coming," Patterson said.

"You're taking a chance too," I said.

Patterson smiled. "You never struck me as a cop killer, DeShawn. Just another lost kid who's run out of options. How old are you?"

"Sixteen."

"How old do you think Marcus Elliot was?"

It might have sounded strange, but I'd never thought about it. "Twenty-seven? Twenty-eight?"

"Try twenty. He would have turned twenty-one next month."

The news surprised me, just as Patterson knew it would.

"It's all about the pose," Patterson said. "But I guess you know that's not what I want to talk about. You know that Jamar's playing both sides against the middle? Making a fortune selling guns and ammo to both the Disciples *and* the Gangstas."

I'd known that for a long time. "How come you don't bust him?"

"Certain people . . . people a lot more cynical than me, seem to think that we're better off letting gang-bangers kill each other. It's a lot cheaper than putting them in jail, and it becomes a problem only when things get out of hand."

"Like when shorties shoot pregnant women?" I said.

"Or innocent bystanders get caught in the cross fire," he said.

"Like my mother."

Patterson nodded. "Mothers, little kids, the kind of stuff that makes the news. And then people have to pretend they're outraged and they're gonna do something about it. That is, until something else comes along and grabs the headlines. People have short attention spans. All it takes is a hurricane or a political scandal to make them forget last week's tragedy. Especially when it comes to the projects. All these young women with two or three children by different fathers. All these fatherless boys running around wild, killing each other. People think it's a shame, but no one really knows how to fix it. So they'd just as soon pretend it doesn't exist."

"If you believe that, why'd you bother becoming a cop?" I asked.

"So I can sleep at night. How you sleeping these days, DeShawn?"

I looked around again, letting Patterson know that I was ready to go.

"We could work together," Patterson said. "No one has to know. You help me take down Rance Jones and his top lieutenants. Then we go after Jamar. You'd be arrested on some fake charge so it wouldn't look like you were the snitch. When the time is right, we could move you, your gramma, sister, and those kids some place new. Some place where you could get a fresh start."

"That's what you're offering me? A fresh start?"

"Marcus Elliott didn't live to be twenty-one," Patterson said. "You're sixteen, DeShawn. How long you think you're gonna last?"

GONE BEFORE DAYLIGHT

Two days later my cell phone rang, and a voice said, "Two a.m. tonight. The parking lot behind King Chicken. Come alone and unarmed. And don't wear no colors."

I did as I was told. It was a cool night, and I wore jeans, a shirt, and that tight, fuzzy blue sweater Gramma had given me for Christmas (so it would be easier to see that I wasn't carrying). When I got there, the parking lot was empty. The moon was almost full, and the smell of fried chicken was in the air. I stood in the middle of the lot with my hands hanging loosely at my sides.

A broad-shouldered figure walked slowly around the side of the building, casting a moonlit shadow, warily looking to the left and right. It was William. He took out a gun. Even in the dark I could tell that it was a Glock.

"Turn around and put your hands against the wall," he said.

I faced the wall and felt the hard end of the gun barrel poke the small of my back. With his free hand William patted me down.

"You alone?" he asked.

"Yeah."

He stepped close, poking the Glock into my ribs. "I ought to shoot you right now," he muttered in a low voice. "What do you think you're doing? Trying to get us both killed?"

"No."

"Then you must be stupid," he snarled. "Seeing my sister, sending word you want to meet Rance. What do you think he's gonna do to me when he figures out what's going on? What do you think he's gonna do to my sister?"

We'd find out soon enough. A black Range Rover slowly pulled into the lot. The windows were as dark as its body, and it had big shiny rims. Still facing the wall, I looked over my shoulder and saw Big D get out of the car. I remembered him from the day they almost shot Snoop. In the moonlight, I could see the tear tattoos at the corner of his eyes.

"Keep facing the wall," he ordered, and slid his hands up and down my arms and legs and around my torso, just as William had a few moments before. These guys weren't taking any chances. When he finished, he clamped a meaty hand on my shoulder and spun me around. He was holding a gun.

"You, me, and William gonna get in that car," he said. "You try anything funny, I'll blow a hole right through your spine."

I started toward the car. William walked ahead, and Big D behind, his gun pressed against my back. When we got to the car, I reached toward the rear door.

"No." Big D poked me. "In the front. Passenger side."

I did as I was told and got in the front. William got into the driver's seat and held the Glock low in his lap, aimed at me. The temptation to turn around and look at Rance was great, but I controlled myself.

Then I smelled something sweet and flowery.

"What the? . . ." William smelled it too, and turned around.

I didn't have to look to know that they had Tanisha. My stomach knotted. Why did they have to bring her into this? But at the same time, I knew exactly why.

"Turn around," a voice said.

I turned. Tanisha was squeezed between Big D and Rance Jones. Rance had grown a goatee since I'd last seen him. Tanisha was wincing, and I could see why: Rance was pressing the barrel of a gun into her ribs.

"Now turn back around so I don't have to look at your ugly Disciple face again," Rance grunted.

I turned and my eyes met William's. His were filled with rage that I had brought this upon his sister and him.

"Talk," Rance said.

"Why'd you have Jamar kill Marcus?" I asked.

A slight gasp came from the backseat, and I suspected that Rance had jabbed the gun harder into Tanisha's ribs. "Who else knows?" he asked. "And tell the truth or she dies."

"One other person," I said.

I heard a click and knew Rance had cocked the gun. "You sure about that?"

A pulse in my forehead throbbed painfully. Every muscle in my body was tense. I heard a sniff and a brief sob, as if Tanisha was trying to fight back tears. But I had to believe Rance wouldn't shoot her. Not with William there. It had to be a bluff.

"Well?" Rance demanded.

"You kill her, and I'll tell the Disciples about Jamar," I said. "You kill me, my friend will tell."

I didn't think a shot would follow, but if it did, I would grab William's gun and kill Rance, or die trying. Because I wouldn't want to live knowing I was responsible for Tanisha's death.

But the shot didn't come. At least not yet.

"Maybe I don't believe you," Rance said. "Give me one good reason why I shouldn't kill you right now."

"You think you're playing Jamar," I said, "but it's the other way around. He's playing you."

There was an uncomfortable silence. In the front seat beside me, William cast an uncertain glance back.

"Keep talking," Rance said.

"Did he and that gun-dealer friend of his try to get you to buy three AK-47s?"

"How . . . ," Rance started to ask, then caught himself. "So what?"

"They had six," I said. "Jamar wanted to make sure the Disciples got the other three."

Silence again. Then Rance said, "Doesn't matter."

"How can it not matter?" I asked. "He's gonna keep selling you and the Disciples ammo and guns and let you keep shooting at each other forever."

"No, he ain't," Rance said. "'Cause there ain't gonna be two gangs much longer."

"Jamar know that?"

"He will when I want him to," Rance said.

"What makes you think you can trust him?"

"He's proved himself."

"By ambushing Marcus?" I said. "What did he have to lose? Now he thinks he's the boss."

"He's done worse."

Darnell, I thought. "That's why he threw that shorty out the window?"

"Not just any shorty," Rance said. "Marcus's nephew. See? He'll do anything I say. And that's all he gotta do. Now that Marcus is gone, there's just gonna be one gang around here. Mine."

I took a deep breath and chose my next words carefully. "There's one thing you need that Jamar can't deliver."

"Oh, yeah? What's that?" Rance sounded amused.

"Loyalty," I said.

Another silence. Then Rance said, "Well, that might just be because there's a rotten apple in the barrel."

I felt the gun against the back of my head. "Get out," Rance said.

"Don't!" I heard Tanisha gasp.

"Shut up," Rance growled.

"Please!"

"Shut your mouth, Tanisha," William grunted. "I told you a hundred times not to mess with this fool. It's your own fault you didn't listen."

The gun was still pressed against my head. I was trembling from head to foot and felt light-headed, like I was going to be sick. Rance had every reason to kill me. This was the end. I was about to become just one more dead gangbanger.

"Get him out," Rance snapped.

William reached across me and pushed open the door. "Out, punk."

"You can't!" Tanisha gasped.

"I said shut it," William grunted.

"I got his baby," Tanisha whispered.

Everything stopped. William twisted around in his seat and stared at his sister. I felt the pressure of the gun barrel slowly ease from the back of my skull.

"You lying to save his sorry butt?" Rance asked.

With the gun no longer pressing against my head, I turned and scowled at her.

She stared back at me with eyes glittery with tears. "It's true."

The shock on my face must have been obvious.

"Ha!" Rance laughed harshly. "Surprise, surprise."

William cursed under his breath.

Tears spilled out of Tanisha's eyes and rolled down her cheeks.

"How come you didn't tell me?" I asked.

"I was going to," Tanisha said with a sniff.

William gave Rance a long, steady look.

"You don't know how lucky you just got, punk," Rance said.

Big D frowned. "You sure?"

"It's gonna be all one gang anyway," Rance said, aiming his gun at my face. I stared down the dark nothingness of the barrel. It was a .45. "You get one chance to prove your loyalty. Mess up and you won't get another, understand?"

I nodded.

Rance gestured at the open car door. "Go home and don't say nothing to no one. The Disciples are gonna find out soon enough anyway. You stay in line and do what you're told, and you and your girl and that little baby'll be okay."

Knowing I was lucky to be alive, I walked home in the moonlight, thinking about Tanisha. *Now what?* I wasn't like Terrell. I couldn't abandon the mother of my child. And that meant there would soon be two more mouths in our family to feed—Tanisha's and the baby's. My fate was sealed. There was only one way I could take care of a family that big.

Ahead, the red and blue lights of police cars flashed. As I got closer to Douglass, I saw a small crowd and bright beams of light sweeping the ground in front of my building. A dozen police officers had cordoned off the area around the bench. Some were keeping people away, while others flashed lights at the building, searching windows for anyone who might want to throw something down on them. Inside the cordoned-off area were men wearing street clothes—detectives—including Patterson.

Lightbulb was leaning against a tree, wearing blue coveralls. He'd recently been fired from King Chicken for not understanding that the customer is always right, even when the customer is wrong. Now he was working the night shift for a janitorial company, washing bathrooms in office buildings from six p.m. to two a.m.

I stopped beside him. "What's going on?"

"Jamar got himself shot," Lightbulb said. He'd grown taller and huskier, and his voice had dropped. But that wasn't the only way he'd changed. He wasn't the same goofy guy anymore. He'd grown quieter and sullen. As if he knew life was passing him by and there was nothing he could do about it.

I felt a chill. "How?"

"Don't know."

But I had a feeling. "You seen Terrell?"

He shook his head. We watched while they wheeled a body bag toward an ambulance parked on Abernathy. The police and detectives stayed bunched together, sweeping their high-powered beams around as they made their way back to their cars. One of the beams swept in my direction, temporarily blinding me. I shielded my eyes and saw a figure step toward me.

"Hey, DeShawn," Patterson said. "How does that

song go? 'Another one bites the dust.' Who do you think's gonna be next?"

I didn't answer. Instead I went inside and up to Terrell's apartment.

"Who is it?" Mrs. Blake asked from inside when I knocked on the door.

"DeShawn."

She came to the door wearing a robe, her hair in curlers. She looked older and more worn-out than ever, but I doubted she was much past thirty-four. Now that Laqueta was dead, the apartment was neat and orderly. Even though it was past two a.m., the TV was on loud.

"Terrell in trouble?" she asked in a low voice.

"No, ma'am," I said. "Is he here?"

She pointed down the hall to his room. I knocked on the dented metal door.

"Who's there?" Terrell called from inside.

The door wasn't locked. I pushed it open. Terrell was sitting at his desk with his feet up and headphones on, playing Grand Theft Auto. He nonchalantly slid the headphones off. "Yo, s'up?"

I closed the door. "Why?"

"Why what?" He pretended he didn't know what I meant.

"You know what I'm talking about," I said. "Where's your gun?"

Terrell quickly glanced at the door. "Keep it down. My momma'll hear."

"She's gonna hear plenty soon enough," I said,

lowering my voice. "Now where is it?"

"Threw it down the sewer," Terrell hissed. "You think I'd be stupid enough to keep it?"

"Why not? You were stupid enough to use it."

Terrell's face hardened. "He killed Marcus. No way he was gonna lead the Disciples. I made sure of that."

"You *tell* anyone he killed Marcus?" I asked.

Terrell shook his head. "You told me not to."

"So when *were* you gonna tell them?"

Terrell didn't answer.

"You didn't just kill Jamar because he killed Marcus," I said. "You killed him to prove to everyone that you can lead the Disciples."

Terrell gazed steadily at me. "So? What's wrong with that? It's a dog-eat-dog world, right? Besides, Jamar deserved it."

"There's just one problem," I said. "Jamar was working for Rance."

Terrell's eyes widened. "For real?" Then his astonishment turned into certainty. He balled his hand into a fist. "Then he *really* deserved it."

"True that," I said. "But what do you think's gonna happen when Rance finds out you killed Jamar?"

Terrell's eyes darted to the left. "But I didn't know."

"You think that'll make a difference?"

My friend's mouth hung open, and his eyes widened. He looked scared. "What am I gonna do?"

A half-open bag of Georgia peanuts lay on the desk. Suddenly I knew the answer. "Go away."

Terrell's eyebrows dipped. "You serious?"

"You stay, I can't guarantee you'll be alive this time tomorrow."

"Where am I gonna go?"

I pointed at the peanut bag and said, "Get packing. You best be gone before daylight."

THE GANGSTA DISCIPLES

The next afternoon, I assembled what was left of the Douglass Disciples in the yard. It was three p.m. and a couple of them were puffy faced, as if they'd just gotten out of bed.

"What's this about?" Jules asked with a yawn.

"The future," I said.

"Where's Terrell?" Bublz asked.

I said I didn't know.

Out on Abernathy the black Range Rover pulled up to the curb. You could feel a change in the air. All over the yard it got quiet. As if everyone knew who that car belonged to. Mothers began pulling their children away. Old folks pushed themselves up with their walkers and canes and started hobbling toward their buildings. Just like those old cowboy movies where the townsfolk scattered when the bad guys rode in. Even before the Range Rover's door opened, Jules was reaching into his jacket.

"Don't," I said.

"But they're Gentry," Bublz sputtered.

"Let's hear what they have to say."

Jules stared suspiciously at me. "How do *you* know they want to talk?"

Big D and William got out first, taking their time and looking around. Antwan got out next. It was the first time I'd seen him since middle school, but I wasn't surprised that he was a Gangsta. Finally Rance got out. With Big D and William in front, he walked slowly toward us. Rance had told me earlier by phone that he wanted to meet outside in the daylight. So everyone could see everyone clearly.

"I come in peace," Rance said.

"The hell you do," Jules challenged him. "After you killed Marcus and Jamar?"

"Didn't kill neither of them," said Rance.

"Then you had them killed," Tyrone said.

Rance shook his head and gestured at me. "Tell them."

"Jamar killed Marcus," I said. "Terrell killed Jamar."

Jules screwed up his face as if he didn't understand. The rest of the Disciples looked stunned.

"Jamar killed Marcus because he wanted to take over the gang," I explained. "Terrell killed Jamar in revenge."

Tyrone looked uncertainly from me to Rance. "What's this all about?"

"Joining forces," Rance said. "What's the point of us killing each other? I need new territory and you need new leadership."

"You expect us to just start wearing Gentry Gangsta colors?" Jules asked defiantly.

"No, I propose a new organization called the Gangsta

Disciples and mix colors," Rance said. "Black and green."

Bublz bit his lip anxiously and gave the rest of us an uncertain look. "What do you think?"

"Like we have a choice," Jules grumbled, and spat on the ground.

"You got a choice in who heads up your part of the organization," Rance said.

That was a smart move. There was a short silence. Then Tyrone nodded at me. "I think it should be you, DeShawn."

SEVENTEEN YEARS OLD

"BEEN SPENDING MOST OF OUR LIVES
LIVING IN A GANGSTA'S PARADISE."
—FROM "GANGSTA'S PARADISE" BY COOLIO

BAD TO THE BONE

The sound of Simon crying in another room woke me. The baby's cries were like a little bird's squawks. Sunlight pressed against the red and green curtains Tanisha had hung over the windows. Still half-asleep, I lay tangled in the deep blue sheets and listened to my son bawl. Simon was three months old. Sometimes I wondered what he would be like. What he would look and act like. Everyone said he would grow up to be good-looking like his parents. If he grew up.

Picking up the heavy, gold Rolex from the night table, I saw that it was 3:54 p.m. I took a bath, then checked myself in the mirror. A few hairs were finally starting to sprout from my chin. Back in the bedroom there was a message on my phone. Rance wanted to see me. I was to come alone. I slipped on some clothes and slid my gun into the waistband holster.

Out in the living room Tanisha was sitting on the couch giving Simon a bottle. Even without makeup she was a beautiful girl. The flat-panel, HDTV was on, and mother and son seemed transfixed by the rapidly changing colors and images.

"Going out," I said. Without taking her eyes from the screen, Tanisha nodded.

Before leaving the fifteenth floor, I went down a few doors and into another apartment. Inside, half a dozen people were sitting at the Ping-Pong table, wearing white masks, filling Baggies with weed and vials with rock. Jules was watching over them. He gave me a nod. Everything was okay.

Back out in the hall, Bublz was sitting at the top of the steps, playing his PSP. Now that the two gangs had joined, we didn't really need a guard, but I kept Bublz up there because there was nothing else he was good for.

On the way downstairs, I stopped to see my family. Gramma and Nia and her new boyfriend, Nathan, were watching TV. Xavier and Jayda were one and a half now. Xavier was sitting on the floor, playing with some plastic blocks. He was a chubby, happy little boy with fat thighs and a round belly, and he always had a big smile for his uncle DeShawn. Jayda was thinner and edgy. She sat next to her mother, sucking her thumb and pressing her pink baby blanket against her face. I rubbed Xavier's head, and he looked up at me and grinned.

Just about everything in the apartment—the TV, the toys, the baby clothes, the food—was there because I'd paid for it.

"What up, bro?" Nathan waved from the couch. He was short and heavyset and happy to eat the food I paid for and watch TV and play video games all day. I nodded tersely, not happy that he was freeloading off my sister. But Nia's belly was big with his baby. And as long as Nia had his baby, he was pretty much staying right where he was.

Gramma looked up from the TV. "You going downstairs?"

"Yep."

"Go over to thirty-one flavors and get me some mint chocolate chip."

"Don't have time."

"Don't give me that," Gramma said. "Just because you a big shot now. I remember changing your stinky Pampers."

Nia gave me a crooked smile. I may have been top dog in the biggest gang in Frederick Douglass, but as far as Gramma was concerned, I was still her gofer.

Outside, the bench was empty. A kid named Arnet was supposed to be there. Feeling anger start to simmer, I spotted him over by the wall chatting up a couple of girls. By the time Arnet saw me coming, it was too late. I smacked him hard, and he stumbled and fell down. The girls backed away to a safe distance.

"I say you could leave the bench?" I asked coldly.

Sitting on the ground, his hand on the side of his head where I'd slapped him, Arnet's eyes darted around as if searching for an escape route. "Ain't no customers."

"Maybe that's 'cause there ain't no one there to sell 'em anything," I snapped. "Get back on that bench."

He jumped to his feet and scurried back. I was about to leave when one of the girls caught my eye. She had long shiny hair, big pretty eyes, glossy lips, and a long, slender body that was easy to imagine beneath her tight jeans and sweater.

"Hi, DeShawn?" she said, slinky-voiced, batting her eyes. "Know who I am?"

"Should I?"

"Sechelle, Lightbulb's sister."

"Lollipop?" I blinked. It was hard to believe that sticky-faced, nappy-haired little girl had grown into such a beauty.

Sechelle pursed her lips. "No one calls me that no more."

Something in me stirred. Now that I was high up in the gang, a lot of women let me know they were interested. So far I'd resisted the temptation, but it wasn't easy.

"Still with Tanisha?" Sechelle asked.

I nodded.

"Bet she's real busy with that new baby," she said. "Gimme your phone."

I handed it to her, and she thumbed in a number and hit save. She handed it back with a smile. "Anytime."

Rance had a club in the basement of one of the Gentry buildings. It had a bar and tables and a dance floor. Just about every night there was loud music and alcohol and drugs and thugs and loose women. Rance spent most of his time in the back room playing cards. The word on the street was that he bet big and lost big.

I parked outside the building. A couple of gang-bangers were leaning on cars. They were Gentry, and even though we were all supposed to be one, big, happy family now, they still gave me suspicious, uncertain looks. Especially Antwan, who wore long braids falling past his shoulders, capped with green beads. He blocked the entrance. "Rance expecting you?"

"That's right," I said.

"Wait here." He went inside.

The hood rats relaxed, but I still felt their eyes on me. A moment later the door opened and Antwan waved me in. The dimly lit club smelled of stale cigarette smoke and spilled beer. The year-round decorations were mostly Christmas lights and tinfoil. A few tables were already occupied by men and women, and at the bar a couple of painted girls gave me the eye. I knocked on the door to the back room.

Big D let me in. The room was small and smoky. Rance and three other men sat around a table, smoking cigars and playing cards. On the table were drinks, handguns, and poker chips. Rance swiveled his head toward me. "Check him, D," he ordered.

I held out my arms. With my jacket open, the gun in my waistband was in plain sight. Big D removed it and held it up for Rance to see.

"Why'd you come in here strapped?" Rance asked while Big D patted down my legs in case I was carrying a second weapon.

"Same reason you did," I said.

"You planning on shooting anyone?" Rance asked.

"If I was, I already would have," I answered.

One of the men at the table chuckled.

"He's clean," Big D said.

"Give me a minute," Rance said, and turned back to the card game. An older man wearing a plaid golf cap won the hand and raked in a pile of chips. Rance told the players to take a break, and they filed out of the room. He pointed his finger at Big D. "You too."

Soon we were alone. At a small bar on the side of the room, Rance reached for a bottle of Johnnie Walker Blue Label and filled two shot glasses. I took a sip. The whiskey burned my throat, and I blinked back tears.

"I hear William ain't happy," Rance said. "He seems to think I'm holding out on him. That what you think too?"

"It's not for me to say," I replied.

"You unhappy with your cut?" Rance asked. "You ever imagine you'd have as much as you got now?"

I shook my head. I'd never imagined it. Not even anything close.

"You like that crib you got? That flat-screen TV and sound system? That nice BMW and all that bling? Your woman or baby wanting for anything?"

Again I shook my head.

"We got a good thing here," Rance said. "Everyone's happy. Things are running smoothly. Nobody shooting nobody. Why let a rotten apple spoil the barrel?" He narrowed one eye. "You know what rotten apple I'm talking about?"

"Uh-huh."

"So how'd you like to make twice what you're making now?" Rance asked. "How'd you like to move out of that low-life project and into a really fresh crib? A place with an elevator that actually works. And an indoor garage for your ride so you don't have to have shorties watching it on the street. A place where you can adjust the heat in the winter and have a toilet that'll flush and a bathroom with a shower. Where you don't get woken up in the middle of the night by screeching train wheels. Nice, huh? Think how much your woman would appreciate getting set up in a place like that."

"That's what you have?" I'd heard he'd moved out of Gentry to another part of town.

"That's right," Rance said. "And you can too. There's just one thing you gotta do."

Rance decided we'd do it that Friday. That was the day he usually met with William and me to divide up the week's money and take care of gang business. On Friday I was just getting into my car when someone yelled, "Hey!"

I looked up. A girl was hurrying toward me with a bunch of books in her arms. She looked familiar. As she got closer, she grinned because she could see I was puzzled.

"Come on," she said.

I took my best guess. "Precious?"

"See, that wasn't so hard," she said, and pointed at my car. "That's a nice whip you got, DeShawn. I'm glad you're gonna give me a ride in it."

"Don't have time."

"Oh, yes, you do," Precious said. "You gangbangers got all the time in the world. Know why? 'Cause you ain't going nowhere. But I am. I'm going to school, and you're giving me a ride because I'm late."

It had been a long time since anyone, except Gramma, had talked to me that way. I could have easily ignored her, or done worse.

Instead I opened the car door for her.

"Since when did you start taking evening classes?" I asked as I drove toward Munson.

"Since I figured out that no Prince Charming was

going to come along and save my sorry butt, so I'd have to do it myself," she said.

We rode in silence while I wondered what my life would have been like if I'd gone to Hewlett Academy or stayed in Munson. I wondered why I was going out of my way to drive Precious to school. Was it because I wanted to believe that someone could make it out of the projects, even if it wasn't me? As if she could read my mind, Precious said, "Know why I knew you'd give me a ride, DeShawn? Because I know you. You may be the top dog around here, but inside you're different. Some of those gangbangers are bad to the bone. But not you. You never were, and you never will be. No matter how hard you try."

I stopped in front of Munson. As Precious got out, she said, "Thanks for the ride. Enjoy your life, DeShawn. Whatever you got left of it."

From there I drove over to Gentry and picked up William. We were equals now. The Disciples reported to me, and the Gentry crew reported to him, and we both reported to Rance. Over the past year, he and I had gradually become more comfortable around each other. There was still some friction left over from the days when Douglass and Gentry were murderous rivals, but we were also family. William wasn't only Tanisha's brother, he was Simon's uncle.

"Any word on how we did this week?" he asked after getting into the car.

"Guess Rance'll tell us," I said as I drove.

"You think?" William said with a heap of sarcasm. "Suppose I told you I've been keeping track of what comes in, and I know for a fact he's keeping a lot more than he's supposed to? And for what? He doesn't do nothing. Just sits in that club all day and plays cards and then goes home to that fancy crib."

"Guess he thinks he earned it," I said.

"For how long?" William asked. "How long do you want to support his lazy butt while he just coasts?"

I didn't answer. William gave me an uncertain look. "You and me are family now. Blood's thicker than water, right? So what if something happens to Rance? Here in the hood things happen all the time. The cops don't care. Another gangbanger gets killed? Good riddance. With Rance gone it would be you and me. And we're blood. Tanisha needs her brother, and Simon needs his father."

Kill or be killed. That's what it always came down to. Nothing to do each day but take care of business and wonder if you'll still be alive in the morning.

"I don't know about you," William went on, "but as far as I'm concerned, today's his last chance. Either he puts up or I'm gonna shut him up for good."

I tensed. "Not in the club."

"You think I'm stupid? He can't stay in that club forever. If things don't get right, some night soon I'll be waiting for him."

At the club, Big D patted both of us down and took

our guns. In the back room Rance was sitting on the couch, watching baseball on TV. He glanced up at me and William.

"Is it that time of the week?" he said. It was a taunt at William. Rance turned back to the TV, purposefully making us wait. "Sorry, boys. I got five g's on Detroit, and it's the bottom of the ninth with one out left."

We waited. The Detroit batter struck out.

"Damn!" Rance muttered. He clicked off the TV. "They clean, Big D?"

"Sure are."

"Okay, you can go," said Rance without rising from the couch.

"How do we know *you're* not carrying?" William asked. It was a stupid thing to say. We'd met like this nearly every Friday for the past year, and William had never said it before. It was an obvious tip off that something was up.

Rance slowly rose from the couch. He gestured at me and said to William, "You trust him?"

William nodded. Rance raised his arms. "Be my guest."

I slid my hands down his body and around his legs. Through the pants, I felt a holster strapped just above his left ankle. The gun in it was stubby with a thick grip. Probably a snub-nosed .38. I glanced up at Rance, and our eyes met in an instant of understanding. It was survival of the fittest. Choosing sides was always a gamble, but sometimes you had no choice. This was one of those times.

"He's clean," I told William.

Rance nodded toward the poker table. "Let's get this over with." He gestured for me to sit on his right and William on his left. Just as he did every week, he unzipped a dark green First National Bank bag and dumped the contents onto the table. Out tumbled neat stacks of bills held with rubber bands. Instantly William and I saw that there was less money on the table than in previous weeks.

Without a word Rance divided the stacks, then leaned back in his chair and crossed his arms. William was glowering.

"Why don't you tell me what's buggin' you," Rance said.

"You know what's buggin' me," William replied.

"You talking about how the shares work?" Rance said as if we didn't know. "The same as always. Each month one third goes to me. You two split one third, and the last third goes to the rest. Ain't nothin' new about that."

"Except it seems like you're taking more than one third," said William. "There's a lot more gwap that comes in than what's on this table right now."

"That's cause you ain't figured in the administrative costs of running this operation," Rance said. "There's a lot of expenses you don't see."

William nodded at the cards and poker chips on the bar. "I think I see one right now."

Rance narrowed his eyes. "I think you see wrong."

"I don't think so," William said. "I think you been losing a lot of our money playin' cards, and my guess is, the cost of that fancy crib of yours also comes out of our share. And I'm saying that from now on, you gotta divide the money up *before* you take out your so-called administrative costs."

Rance glanced at me, then shook his head slowly. "I don't think that's gonna happen."

"DeShawn and I think it should," William replied.

Rance gave me a feigned look of surprise. "Is that so?"

That was my cue. I reached under the chair where the gun was taped, pulled it out, and aimed it at William, whose jaw dropped and eyes bulged. Rance seemed pleased by the result. "See, there are certain things you don't understand, William," he said. "I worked hard to get where I am. Every gangbanger I started out with is dead or in jail. I'm the only one left. And that means I've earned certain privileges. I'm in charge of this gang. I handle the finances. I decide what the administrative costs are. And . . . I decide who lives and dies."

William was trembling. "I . . . I thought we were blood," he stammered to me.

Rance laughed harshly. "Blood? That don't mean

nothin'. Where you been, boy? This is about money. It's about who gets what. And too bad for you, it looks like from now on, your share's going to someone else." He nodded at me. "Do it."

I slipped off the safety and looked into William's wide eyes. "DeShawn," he whimpered. "How you gonna face Tanisha?"

"Don't be stupid," Rance chuckled haughtily. "DeShawn's gonna be second in command of the Gangsta Disciples. He don't have to worry about facing no one. They gonna have to worry about facing him." He looked at me again. "Now do it, boy. You want it, you gotta earn it."

Keeping the gun aimed at William, I turned my head and stared at Rance.

"You want an equal share, do it," he ordered.

I swung my arm around and aimed the gun at him. "You killed LaRue. Father of my sister's babies. Here's how I get my equal share."

Rance's eyes widened. He reached for his ankle.

I pulled the trigger. *Bang!*

Rance fell back and tumbled to the floor with a thud. I got up and stood behind the door as Big D burst in, gun drawn. By the time he saw Rance lying in a pool of blood, the barrel of my gun was pressed against the back of his skull. Big D raised his hands. William took the gun from him.

Antwan and some of the hood rats raced in next

with their guns drawn. I held my gun to Big D's head. "Drop 'em."

Guns clattered to the floor.

"Rance had an accident," I said calmly. "William and I are the leaders of this gang from now on. Everyone understand?"

Big D nodded slowly. The others followed his example.

"Whatever he was paying you, we'll pay you more," I said. "Big D, how's that sound to you?"

"Good," the big man said.

"You sure?" I asked.

Big D nodded at Rance's body. "Never liked that man. He was as mean and nasty as they come."

I lowered my gun. "What kind of ride you got, Big D?"

"Well, I ain't actually rollin' right now," he said.

"How'd you like a Range Rover?" I asked.

"Serious?" Big D gasped.

I pointed at Rance's body. "I think you'll find the keys and registration on him. And take whatever cash is in his wallet and share it with these fellows."

"Yes, sir," Big D said. "Thank you, sir."

"And from now on, if anyone asks who's running this gang?" I said.

"You two," said Big D.

TWENTY-EIGHT YEARS OLD

Recent studies have shown that the huge pool of poorly educated black men is becoming ever more disconnected from mainstream society, especially in the country's inner cities where work is scarcer than ever and prison is routine.

In 1995, 1,585,400 people were in American jails. By 2005 that number had increased to 2,320,359.

Three times more black men live in jail cells than in college dorms.

"WE ALL GONNA DIE SOMEDAY
SO, DIE HUSTLIN FOR YOURSELF
OR DIE HUSTLIN FOR MILLIONS OF YOUR PEOPLE."
—FROM "FO DA MONEY" BY COUP

PRISON

Four months later, a week after I turned eighteen, I was picked up and charged with the murder of Rance Jones. They also got me for racketeering, money laundering, and drug and weapons trafficking. Before I killed him, Rance had made a deal with the cops, and the back room of the club had been wired with video. It was supposed to have shown me killing William. That way Rance would have gotten rid of both of us.

Instead it showed me killing Rance. And thanks to the video, the cops didn't need the testimony of any snitches.

That was ten years ago. Today I sit in a prison cell, where I will almost surely spend the rest of my life. For much of each day, my view of the outside world is through a narrow sliver of window six inches wide and two feet tall. I will never get to play with Simon. I will never feel the softness of Tanisha's skin. I will never eat a steak or good crispy french fries or a milk shake again. Compared to this, living in the Frederick Douglass Project was paradise.

Do I wish I'd listened to Mr. Brand and my other

teachers and done things differently? Darn right, I do. But that's one of the biggest problems impoverished, young black men face in the hood. We don't know who to believe or trust or listen to.

According to statistics, black Americans represent 13 percent of the overall population in this country, but we make up 50 percent of the prison population. Many of the young men who get sent here were in gangs on the outside, and they join them on the inside, because there are gangs in here, too. Just like on the outside, these young men feel they have no choice and are afraid of what will happen to them if they don't join.

Is our situation hopeless? Sometimes it feels that way. But I cling to the idea that there is hope in education. Not necessarily the "education" they're giving inner-city kids in schools today, but an education that relates to their lives; one that helps them understand why their world is the way it is, and what they can do to change it. If kids understood why their parents and older brothers and sisters can't find work, and why so many take drugs and join gangs, then maybe we could begin to educate our way out of poverty and self-destruction.

But I also know that this isn't a problem that's going to be solved overnight. It's going to take generations. It's going to take vast amounts of money. It's going to take a government that is willing to acknowledge the overwhelming failure of this country's inner-city public schools, and is willing to dedicate a larger part of its energies and resources to rebuilding them.

I still hear from some of the folks from my past. Detective Patterson's retired. But he writes me letters now and then, mostly about what his grandchildren are up to. He's also written to the parole board on my behalf. But he says I shouldn't get my hopes up.

I hear from Nia. The twins are almost twelve, and her daughter DeShawna is almost ten. They're all in school, which is good. Nathan's long gone. Gramma still spends most of her days in front of the TV. Lightbulb writes now and then. He still lives with his momma and works as a janitor. Probably will for the rest of his life. Last time he wrote, he said Sechelle had some kids but they were put in foster homes because she was messed up on drugs.

Darius got out of prison and became a recording engineer. He's worked with some semifamous rap stars. Tanisha is a saleswoman in a department store. She's married, but she sends me photos and news about Simon. She's a good woman, and I miss her. Precious is a registered nurse. Ms. Rodriguez is *still* an assistant principal.

So a few made it, but just about every other guy I grew up with is either dead or in prison. You get plenty of time to think in here, and sometimes I wonder what my life would have been like if I'd been born in a small town or some nice suburb. If I had, how many of my friends would have been murdered? How many would have wound up in jail?

There's one other person I hear from:

Yo DeShawn,

So how they treet you up there? Ok, I hope. Things is good here. Dawn Mae is pregnant with our 3rd baby. She's really hoping for a girl now that we got 2 boys. Thomas is going into 2nd grade. Jason's in Kintergaterten. They are a couple of raskels.

I'm still workin' my but off on the farm. After all those years being inside so much, I love being outside. Even when it's 110 and swets poorin off you like a waterfall. We put in a good crop this year and made some money. Dawn Mae says maybe it time for us to buy a house.

That detective stil trying to help you with parole? I hope so. Strange how things work out, ain't it? If someone asked me back in the day which one be married with kids and a job? And which be in jail? I'd have bet for sure it would be the other way round.

So that's all for now. Keep the faith, bro. I still got your back.

Terrell.

NOTES

My sources for this book were many and varied and included conversations with gang members and residents of projects in and around the New York City area.

The following four books were helpful:

There Are No Children Here: The Story of Two Boys Growing Up in the Other America by Alex Kotlowitz. New York: Anchor Books, 1991.

Random Family: Love, Drugs, Trouble, and Coming of Age in the Bronx by Adrian Nicole LeBlanc. New York: Scribner, 2003.

The Shame of the Nation: The Restoration of Apartheid Schooling in America by Jonathan Kozol. New York: Crown, 2005.

The American Street Gang: Its Nature, Prevalence and Control by Malcolm W. Klein. New York: Oxford University Press, 1995.

In addition, I used dozens of newspaper and magazine articles. The following three stand out in my mind:

"An Economic Analysis of a Drug-Selling Gang's Finances" by Steven D. Levitt and Sudhir Alladi Venkatesh in the *Quarterly Journal of Economics*, August 2000.

"A Poverty of the Mind" by Orlando Patterson in the *New York Times*, March 26, 2006.

"Preventing Adolescent Gang Involvement" by Finn-Aage Esbensen in the *Juvenile Justice Bulletin*, September 2002.

There is a great deal of information about gangs on the Internet. Two of the best organized and most thorough sites I visited were:

Street Gangs resource center at http://www.streetgangs. com (This offers a large bibliography on gang culture.)

Office of Juvenile Justice and Delinquency Prevention at http://www.ojjdp.ncjrs.org

ABOUT THE AUTHOR

Todd Strasser has written many award-winning novels, including *Boot Camp, Can't Get There from Here, Give a Boy a Gun,* and *How I Created My Own Prom Date,* which was adapted for the Fox feature film *Drive Me Crazy.* He decided to write *If I Grow Up* after visiting several inner-city schools and reading about the growing problem of gangs. Strasser frequently speaks at schools about the craft of writing and conducts writing workshops for young people. He lives in a suburb of New York City.

PETE
HAUTMAN

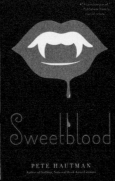

PRINT AND EBOOK EDITIONS AVAILABLE

It was like being in a car with the gas pedal slammed down to the floor and nothing to do but hold on and pretend to have some semblance of control. But control was something I'd lost a long time ago

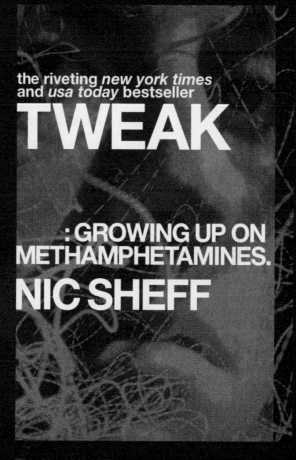

the riveting *new york times* and *usa today* bestseller

TWEAK

: GROWING UP ON METHAMPHETAMINES.

NIC SHEFF

The *New York Times* bestselling memoir of one meth addict's descent into darkness and his subsequent road to recovery.

From Atheneum Books for Young Readers. Published by Simon & Schuster. EBOOK EDITION ALSO AVAILABLE.